SILK

SILK

stories by

Grace Dane Mazur

Grace Dane Mazur

For Ernest —
who knows the joy
of writing.
Grace Dane Mazur
25 March 2003

Lumen Editions
a division of Brookline Books

ISBN 1-57129-028-1

Library of Congress Cataloging-In-Publication Data
Mazur, Grace Dane.
    Silk : stories / by Grace Dane Mazur.
       p.   cm.
    ISBN 1-57129-028-1 (pbk).
    I. Title.
PS3563.A9872S56   1996
813'.54--dc20   96-26941
                                          CIP

Published by:
Lumen Editions
Brookline Books
P.O. Box 1047
Cambridge, Massachusetts 02238

For Barry,
Zeke, and Heather.

Contents

Acknowledgments

I am grateful to Charles Baxter, Robert Boswell, Ali Dor-Ner, Helen Fremont, C.J. Hribal, Margot Livesey, Fred Marchant, Barry Mazur, Sadi Ranson, Mary Elsie Robertson, Rick Russo, John Skoyles, Carol Houck Smith, Ellen Bryant Voigt, and C.K. Williams.

Privacy

THE SUNSWEPT GRAVEYARD WAS ITCHY WITH DARK DRESSES and white lace collars; everyone who kissed me smelled of mothballs. All the grown-ups seemed to lean slightly in the wind as they stood around Grandfather's silver-handled coffin. Everyone stood dark and still beside the open grave, except for my aunt Marika who wore one of her flowing dresses of yellow linen and a yellow straw hat; she was edging her way back through the mourners until she reached the outer wall of the cemetery. As I slipped away to follow her, my mother tapped the side of her thigh in an unmistakable gesture telling me to come back to my place and be still. I pretended not to understand.

"Marika," I whispered when I finally caught up to her. "Where are you going? Can I come?"

She didn't answer, so I followed.

In those days we went to the south of France every summer, to see my father's family in the Dordogne. This was our last visit. I was ten.

Marika and I left the cemetery and walked along the side of the road. She took her shoes off and put them in her handbag. Then she started gathering flowers: daisies and blood-red poppies and yellow tasselled blooms that looked to me like weeds. I helped her.

"Why are we doing this?" I asked at last.

No reply. I looked at her to see if she was weeping, but she seemed intent rather than sad.

I asked her, "Is this what we are supposed to be doing?" I knew it wasn't, but I wanted to get my bearings.

When our arms were full of flowers we made our way back to the graveyard. People stood as before. No progress had been made in our absence.

For the next two weeks the verandah clinked and muttered with tea cups and quiet visitors.

The days of those Dordogne summers were long and swollen with heat. There were never any other kids my age. Ours was a family which loved privacy—for which there is no word in the French language—and, after gathering for meals at the long dark dining table, parents and grandparents, aunts and uncles and cousins would take themselves off to their own secret doings.

I would breakfast early, before anyone but Hermine, the cook, was up. In the kitchen, she would set a bowl of hot chocolate on a wooden tray, along with a piece of thick gray bread smeared with butter and strawberry jam. Then I would make the dawn journey to the dining room, avoiding the coiled beasts who lay in the red parts of the Persian carpet. I navigated with my tray around the small tables of polished wood, the steaming chocolate sloshing in my green bowl.

Some days the red terrain of the rug was not beasts at all, but a sort of swamp or quicksand which could catch me by the legs and keep me half in and half out of the rug, neither holding me nor letting me go. No other place in the house of my grandparents shimmered with danger as did this carpet on the way to the dining room in the very early morning.

In previous summers my grandfather would often join me at breakfast and the two of us would speak in whispers in the semi-dusk of the dark-paneled room, as though we were conspiring.

My grandmother was up early, taking her tray of coffee and toast to the stone wall where she left it balanced while she gathered figs from the ancient tree in the corner. Then she carried everything to the table on the verandah and sat there writing letters, stopping only to brush away an occasional wasp which had darted down from the overhanging grapes. Sometimes, if I passed too close, she would grab my wrist and pull me to her, in order to lecture me about something. "Listen to me, Cass," she said one day, "Letter writing will die out altogether if no one will give it a morning." I stood there quietly, enveloped in her scent of lavender water and face powder. As she talked I played with the silver combs in her white hair, and she cajoled me about my own hair, tugging at it fondly as though to make it grow more quickly. I was fiercely tomboyish and kept my too-red hair clipped short—except for my bangs, which everyone thought were too long—hacking away at it myself when my mother was too slow to cut it. I also had a habit of holding onto my crotch. Grandmother did not like that.

∞

My aunt Marika was about ten years younger than my mother,

and left Poland when my mother did, in the late 1930's, my mother eventually going on to the States, and Marika settling in Paris. Both women were red-haired though my mother was lean while Marika was full and spontaneous. The clothes Marika wore during her visits to the south were like the fields in summer: muted orange and olive and soft dark yellows usually of linen. When it was cool in the evening she would wear two or three blouses over one another, and two skirts, say, an orange one with a white underskirt.

My father's mother clearly enjoyed Marika's presence and would invite her to come down from Paris and spend each summer with us. Granny seemed to expect Marika to behave differently from her own brood, and would often give a hopeless and loving smile, saying: "*Ah Marika: esprit de peintre, esprit de travers.*" The mind of the artist runs at cross purposes.

Aunt Marika was never considered 'correct' by the rest of the family. She went barefoot around the house. Otherwise, she said, the little toe would atrophy from disuse, leaving future generations to be born with only four toes—she had a Lamarkian view of evolution. Marika's lack of a husband was taken by my father's family as another sign of perverseness. There were rumors of lovers, but she always showed up in those Dordogne summers alone. Finally, the family thought that painting was something one didn't do, not seriously. Museum work was fine, both of my parents did that, but for Marika to be a painter was at the farther limit of behavior. I was discovering that the world was full of such lines, faint as gossamer in the forest, and I often wouldn't know I had tangled with one until a grown-up called out to me with that special emphatic hesitation, "Ah, Cass. One doesn't... run about so wildly." And if I happened to be still, someone was sure to say, "Cass, hold yourself properly," meaning that I shouldn't hold myself at all. How they all lectured me; it was as if my presence triggered some corrective reflex. Injunctions proliferated as though by spontaneous generation. Any passing adult had the right to tell me, "Et *les coudes*..." And the elbows. Which were supposed to be glued to my sides: only hands and forearms were allowed to gesture, as though there was a fear of coming unstuck. I never talked back to adults in France. I liked being there—though I was on the look-out, raw-skinned and watching.

My father, Pierre, still considered himself French, although he had lived in Boston for almost twenty years. Frenchness is something you don't lose, he told me. It seemed to be something my mother couldn't find, either. She considered herself American and had completely suppressed her Polish accent, I suspect by taking voice lessons. Her French, though, was always tortured and accented. My older brother Thomas and I had both been born in the States. He was in college and too old to still come on family trips, though he showed up briefly for my Grandfather's funeral.

At that time I spoke a correct and childish French, but whenever I tried to copy the slangy talk of my older cousins Granny would pounce on it with a smile, repeating my bold words to anyone who would listen, calling ridicule down on me like summer flies. "One mustn't descend into vulgarity," she said. "It always sounds out of place in the mouths of foreigners."

∞

The cellar of my grandparents house was a huge room cut out

of limestone. On hot days I would spend time sitting on the cool stone steps, in that summery mental state of not-quite-thinking. A cistern in the corner had a special pump which would kick on with a startling whine. Grandfather had rigged it up and when he took it apart to clean it he would show me its innards and valves. Sometimes we would take walks in the forest together, and he would teach me how to cup my hands over the transparent-winged bronze-colored cicadas in the pine trees. He told me about their 17-year life cycle, and with his pocket knife he pried up bark to reveal a cache of their eggs. Then he let me dig with the blade in the dirt under the pines until I found the larvae and nymphs bur-rowed underground.

Grandfather also told me about the importance of cellars as security, showing me a hidden room he had constructed out of wooden planks and rubble during the war. There he had concealed most of the conserves and the wine, leaving only a few jars and bottles in the visible part of the cellar in case the German troops came so far south. I knew that my mother and Marika had been harbored and hidden by a French family in a village further to the east.

The cellar was divided into territories. My father and his two brothers would buy wine for their families and store it there. Granny was in charge of all the food. When she made *confits* of goose or duck, plump pieces cooked and preserved in fat, she would paste an octagonal label on each glass jar, and write on it in her angular script with an ink pen: *Confit d'Oie, Été, 1965. Pour Pierre et famille.* Goose Preserve, Sum-mer, 1965. For Pierre and family. Or: *Gelée de Coings, Été, 1966. Pour Marika.* Quince Jelly, Summer, 1966. For Marika.

Sometimes I would take a jar of amber jelly and roll it back and forth over my cheeks and my forehead.

One afternoon that last summer, as I ran my fingers along the black currant conserves, I noticed circles in the dust at the end of the shelf, prints from jars that had been taken. I didn't remember seeing so many empty circles and it seemed that some anxious message was waiting to be read there. Using a pencil from Grandfather's workbench, I made some calculations on the stone wall, trying to see if we were going through the shelves faster than Granny was filling them. Finally I sat down on the old horsehair mattress which had recently found its way down from one of the attic rooms. It was covered with a maroon blanket. Occasionally someone would have taken the mattress into Grandfather's workroom, and then I would drag it back to my spot, near the preserves. A few days later I would find it in the workroom again. It didn't occur to me, then, to ask myself who else was using it, or why.

Remembering, now, that the workroom door could be locked from the inside, I try to read the rumpled folds of the dark red blanket, and to recall what, or who, it smelled of, besides attic dust and mold from the cellar. Along with the upheaval and grief caused by my grandfather's death, that summer was full of erotic turbulence. I am sure of this now, but then I was so young that all I saw were a few eddies at the margins—like the continual wandering of the mattress I considered mine.

That day, in the cellar, I lay back on the lumpy horsehair to look at the shelves and everything appeared peculiarly empty. Grandfather's pump gave a click and then a high pitched wheeze. I thought I could smell again that musky black smoke of his cigarettes mixed with pine resin and the flinty odor of honed edges which always seemed to hover about him. The new pain of missing him startled me. His death meant that now I was alone, marooned in the corrective and admonishing world of women. Of course that wasn't technically true, my father and uncles were there, and my older cousins, but they rarely said anything to me. Grandfather had shown me how certain pieces of the universe fit together, without using it as an occasion for the reform of my person. He never straightened me or told me to get my hair out of my eyes. Alone, I looked at the shelves and saw only absence and change. Grandmother had stayed in bed for several mornings that week, saying that she had reading to catch up on. The aunts had said it was exhaustion and grief, but I wasn't sure. What if she were dying? The world was shaky. I would have to become self-sufficient, taking all my food directly from the outdoors, living only on what I could catch and gather. I decided, at that moment, to become a hunter.

At the end of the shelf were heaps of thin black dried mushrooms which Grandfather and I had gathered at the end of the previous summer. As I took them in my hands their sinewy toughness reminded me of small creatures with dark animal smells chittering about the forest.

I had my pocket knife, string and a box of matches. There was no one I wanted with me: my brother Thomas had left; the younger cousins were too small; the older ones were teenagers and kept themselves apart. They had their own explosive conversations, about motorbikes and *boums*, which were dancing parties, and *terminale*, which meant the last year of high school, but had an ominous sound.

I had to make arrows that afternoon: the following day the uncles were going to take us to one of the pre-historic caves nearby. Granny's friend Marion, an old lady who worked on cave paintings, was going to guide us. It had been three weeks since Grandfather's funeral; the grown-ups said we needed an excursion to cheer us up. Perhaps they needed one, too.

Softly, I closed the cellar door behind me and stepped outside into the yellow hush of afternoon heat. The mid-summer grass stretched in front of me, shivery and wild.

At the edge of the woods I found a long stick and whittled its tip to make a spear, shaving through the green underbark to the fragrant whitewood. I practiced throws. For a bow, I cut a sapling and tied it with my string. All the sticks I found were too bent or knobby for arrows so I decided to search by the river. I glided through the forest, practicing silence.

The forest pulsed with its own noises. Cicadas drilled through the swell of the heat. At times it seemed as though they all stopped, and then took up again, in unison. I wondered if they had really ceased or if I had forgotten to listen. Flies inspected my face and then took off; honeybees from Grandfather's hives droned among purple thistles as high as my head. A breeze hit the top of the pines making them whisper. A pair of magpies swooped over a nearby field skimming the grass in parallel. A cuckoo called its clear-voiced taunt while other birds chattered from the scrub. I looked about for lizards.

Far off I could hear Clio barking. She had been Grandfather's hunting dog, and would always come when the old man took me on expeditions in the forest. She was large and rough, obedient to no one now that Grandfather was dead. I kept as far away from her as possible.

I crept down to the shiny-leafed bushes by the edge of the water. It was not really a river, but a broad stream which fed into the Dordogne River some kilometers away. Downstream my cousins had dammed it with rocks to make a swimming hole, but here, where the reeds grew, trees and bushes grew right at the banks. No one came here because it was so shallow. Old willows on the opposite side spread their branches over the water and made a hollow of greenish gloom.

Something large was moving slowly through the field at the edge of the woods; I cursed myself for not having any arrows. I tried to figure out if herons ever wandered so far from the water. Grandfather had told me that although their flesh was leathery and had a powerful stench, they could be eaten. I calculated that I could live for two weeks on the meat of one heron, if I had some means of preserving it.

Marika.

I was disappointed. Beside her trotted the black and white pointer, Clio.

I stalked them, woman and dog, stepping carefully to keep dry leaves from crackling. I hoped the droning of the cicadas would cover me. Marika's blouse was beige and full; her olive green skirt billowed as she walked. She stopped beside the stream and put down her easel, which was still screwed into a small bundle. Her wooden paint box she placed on the bank beside it. Other summers she had let me settle beside her when she painted in the fields, but recently she had turned moody, chasing me from her, saying, "No, my girl, off with you: today I hunt my landscapes alone."

I crawled under a dense shrub. Marika smoothed her blouse, then took the pins out of her hair which showered free, fiery in the sun, full of waves and frizzes. Leaning back a little, she combed it with her fingers, then coiled it up again, pinning it into one of her strange knots. She whistled to the dog. Clio looked back at her, then continued sniffing along the edge of the stream.

Taking off her sandals Marika glanced around as if to make sure no one was about. Then she lifted up her voluminous skirt and tucked it into her wide leather belt. Underneath she was stark naked.

I gasped. I had never considered what she or any of my other aunts would be wearing under their clothes, but I was certain they wore something. They certainly made a fuss when I didn't. Yet here was Marika, her pubic hair an astonishing yellow-gold, her ample white hips and bottom naked.

She began walking out onto the largest of the willow branches which extended just above the water. When she got out over the stream, she did something I have never been able to understand: holding onto one of the branches above, and standing on the lowest one, she dipped her buttocks into the water. Immediately she jumped up again, stifling a small cry. Clio trotted over, yapping excitedly. Marika lowered herself again, shuddered once, and this time kept her bottom submerged. She swayed back and forth.

At first it was only my fear of being caught spying that kept me there in my hiding place. Soon fascination took over. I watched Marika swaying from the willow branches, half-naked, glistening and blushing, in and out of the dappled water. She was humming to herself. Listening to her, I discovered a strange inverse kind of longing. For, if normal longing is desire without an object, there, with Marika half-nude in the stream, I had an object, but no precise desire. I didn't know then what I was feeling. I'm not sure I know now. I had been told, by each of my parents, secretly and separately, about the hidden geometries of sex and conception, but they had not told me about yearning, or desire for understanding, or such terror born of mystery. Of course, while observing Marika I held onto my crotch, but for me, then, that was a reflex gesture of wonder or fear.

I watched Marika. Her skin glowed pink and gold under the clear water. I couldn't quite hear what she was singing. I shifted a bit and a twig snapped. Clio stared directly at my hiding place. She stiffened and began to point, her head and gaze rigid, her tail straight out, and her forepaw raised and curled backwards.

Noting the dog's sudden change Marika whistled to her, and called, "Oh, Clio, it's just a bird, just a bird in the bushes. Relax, my dear. *Calme-toi.*"

But when Clio stayed in position, so tense that she was on the verge of quivering all over, Marika hoisted herself up, shuddered, and, with her skirts still raised, turned gingerly on her branch and looked in my direction.

Cicadas roared. Birds shrilled warnings to each other, about the dog, about the hidden girl. Marika squinted into the sun,

shading her eyes with one hand. The sun had turned feverish. My skin prickled.

Finally she shrugged and turned towards the dog. "Clio,
my dear, I think we've done enough for today, don't you?"
Clio barked once and relaxed her pose.

When they had gone, I came out of my hiding place and
sat at on the coarse dry grass by the water's edge, laying my
newly carved spear and bow beside me. My throat felt rasped
and swollen. My eyes stung. I peeled off my t-shirt, shorts
and underpants and walked into the stream.

The cold was like a slap. I wanted to howl but didn't
dare. I lay down and pulled myself along, keeping my hands
on the bottom until I was floating near the willows. The grit
and stones of the stream bed felt solid and good. I moved
quietly in the shade, making hardly a ripple, the cold line of
the water's surface slicing just above my lips. Under the willows I kneeled and took handfuls of river gravel, lifting it out
of the water and letting it play between my fingers as it fell
back in. Rhythmically dipping my head into the stream I
blew bubbles again and again.

As I clambered out of the river, numb with cold, I thought
back to Grandmother's tirade at lunch. She had been furious
because the older cousins had closed the chicken house door
after some of their mischief. One of the hens had been trapped
there when the rat attacked.

"No one must ever latch that hen house door," she said,
"No one."

I watched her veiny hand beat the air in time with her
speech. She stressed that the blond hen had been brooding
when the rat came, but could not escape because of the closed

door, and, as we could imagine, what followed was *"massacre et carnage."* I rolled the French words around in my mouth like hard candies. In English, it seemed better reversed: "carnage and slaughter." It had been her favorite hen, like a blond pheasant, all tan and white, round-bellied and proud, with a long white tail.

Granny's vehemence delighted me. It seemed to fit well with the taste of the raspberries we were having for dessert. We all stopped eating and watched her. As the blast of her anger spread I thought I could smell lavender water and powder. I wondered why she glared about so, not at my cousins, the traditional wrongdoers, but at my aunts and uncles, and particularly at my father. I must have known even then that it wasn't just a question of chickens.

Marika had not come to lunch. Her chair stood empty and dark, her place untouched. My father, who always poured the wine, must have suspected she wasn't coming, as he had not filled her glass. When Granny stopped speaking, my mother asked to be excused; she left the table suddenly and hurried into the garden. My father folded his napkin and ran out after her. The rest of the family, subdued, became suddenly interested in raspberries and cream. Hermine, the cook, brought in the coffee tray a little early, as though she wanted to see what was going on. This all made no sense to me then, yet now the hidden algebra seems so simple it's hardly even a calculation.

I put on my t-shirt and shorts and cut my arrows from bamboo growing along the stream. Then I padded through the forest with an arrow notched on my bowstring. In the caves of the region I had seen paintings of reindeer and bison and low-bellied horses, but I knew I would find only birds or lizards or those strange reddish French squirrels with devil-like tufts by the ears.

A rabbit.

Of course I missed it. It startled me, appearing suddenly at the turning. I had been looking up, dazzled by golden sunlight filtering through the treetops; my arrow arced crazily over a bush. The odd thing was, when I found the arrow in the path beyond the turn, there was a rabbit beside it, a dead one. I was sure I had not hit it. I wondered if it had died of fright. I inspected the body for arrow wounds and sniffed it: rather like guinea pig, not at all spoiled. At the time, I accepted its presence as a simple coincidence—something I needed had appeared—and didn't question it; now, looking back, the sudden materializing of a dead rabbit, just then, seems impossible and strange.

I picked it up by the hind legs, deciding that I would skin it, for practice, but not eat it. A rabbit stretched full length can be quite long; I had to hold my arm up to keep the front paws from dragging on the ground as I searched for a good place to sit. When my right arm ached, I switched it to my left, then I draped the body around my neck like a scarf, with the head and forelegs on one side, the hind legs on the other. At first the white fur of the belly was soft against my neck. Soon we both became hot and sweaty.

I settled against the trunk of a large oak, the animal on the ground between my legs. Remembering the skinned rabbits with their furry paws hanging in the window of the butcher shop, I tried to cut neat slits around the back feet, but my knife kept slipping against the resiliency of skin and fur. The rabbit's blood was suddenly everywhere, reddening the ground. The shock of so much red got in the way of breathing. I hiccuped. I hadn't thought about how much an animal would bleed. Red smears covered my hands and arms as I tried to work my blade under the fur. The forest was quiet. Except for my hiccups. I rubbed my hands on the ground to get the blood off, but dirt stuck to the crimson patches. Leaning back and scratching my shoulders against the tree I hiccuped and I wondered why Marika had peered so long in my direction: because she had seen me? or because she had not?

The blood dried to a reddish-brown coating on my hands and arms. I gave up trying to skin the animal; there were knife moves that would make the whole operation simple, but I didn't know them. Sometimes Hermine bought freshly killed rabbits from a local farmer; she could teach me what to do. Meanwhile, I wanted to bury this one. The dirt proved too dry and hard to dig, so I placed it beside a laurel bush. I gathered chunks of ochre-colored limestone, arranging them in a circle and covered the body with laurel leaves. I drove my spear into the ground near the rabbit's head.

As I walked home, the idea of facing Marika at dinner bothered me. I thought of saying I didn't feel well, or simply not showing up. I hid my weapons in the stone wall at the end of the lower garden and scuffed through the grass on my way to the house. Clio bounded towards me, barking. Suddenly her voice changed. She stiffened a moment, pointed, and finally broke position, leaping at me and pushing me over backwards. I yelled at her in English, then, remembering where I was, in French.

Clio stood on me, growling, her teeth by my cheek. She clawed at my arms. Her paws drilled down on me. She smelled of swamp and drool. I rolled over onto my stomach and crossed my hands over my head, moaning.

Hermine burst out from the kitchen. She snapped her dish towel, cracking it on Clio's rump, shooing the dog away. "But why didn't you call me, idiotic little goose? Just lying there with that animal on top of you." She pulled me up. "Look at you: you're covered with blood. Let's go, we'll take you inside and wash you."

In a whisper I told her about the rabbit and said that Clio had probably been after the blood on me, or playing some kind of game.

"It didn't look like any game to me," she said, brushing grass and dirt off my clothes. "Why are you whispering?" she asked. "Did she bite you?"

I had no idea why I wasn't talking out loud. I shook my head, then spat on my arms and wiped them to show her. "Just scratches," I said finally, in my normal voice. I watched the new blood pooling in parallel claw marks.

While Hermine was scrubbing my arms with soap Grandmother came into the kitchen. She took over. She rinsed me under the faucet, then held me firmly by the wrists and examined my arms. "Gentian Violet is what we need," she said, looking through the bottles in the cabinet by the sink. She painted stinging and brilliant purple stripes on each arm. "There you are, Apache warrior. Run quickly, now. Wash your face and get into some decent clothes for dinner. No bandages, I think. It's best to leave some things uncovered."

∽

At dinner, the long table was set with a white cloth and crystal. Silver candlesticks held yellow beeswax candles. Grandmother told my father to put some red wine in my glass—'*pour la fortifier,*' to make her stronger, she explained. "Don't forget to cut it with a little water," she added.

The aunts and uncles and cousins were all seated, everyone except my mother. As I took my place, Marika gave me a smile which seemed to have no new history behind it. I slipped into my chair, weak with relief. I smiled back at her and remembered her half nakedness in the stream, just that part which was obscured now by the edge of the tablecloth. I thought of her skin, rosy and shimmering in the reflections from the water. I blushed and quickly turned away to look at my father. But I had seen him naked, too. Not often, but enough so that it was easy to imagine him dark and hairy and surprising under the table. My mother appeared as we were starting the soup. She too had a body, now, under her dress, and my mind stripped her as she walked, with the stiffness of new sadness, to her chair. Her skin was darker than Marika's, her small-breasted body seemed brittle and defenseless. I felt I was wronging her to have such a clear view of her. No one was safe: wherever I rested my eyes, there were nude bodies, their clothes just flimsy tissue easily ripped off by my vision. I looked around me, feeling furiously hot and red, sure that I was going to be found out.

Granny was directing a question to me, but I was so pre-occupied with the intensity of seeing that I couldn't focus on hearing, until finally my father reached over, took my plate, and handed it to her saying, "Of course Cass wants some chicken with forest mushrooms."

Granny asked, still patient but amused, "Which part, little one?"

All I could think of was crotch, groin, buttocks. How strange all those words sounded. I knew the French cut up their chickens differently from the way we do, and I couldn't recall if they even used our terms, *breast, leg, thigh*. I couldn't think of a single French word. Or of anything that made sense. I realized that I'd never seen a rooster's penis and this felt important. I wondered if they had them. I examined my teenage cousins down at the other end of the table and they became a raucous heap, teeming with breasts and thighs and legs, testicles and penises.

Granny tapped the prongs of her silver serving fork against the platter. She gave me her quizzical look.

"*Oui. S'il vous plait. Grandmère,*" I croaked, my voice not much more under control than my mind.

She laughed and said, "*Eh bien. Voilà une cuisse.*" Well, here's a thigh, then.

As my father went around the table pouring wine, he held forth on the cave we would visit with Granny's friend from Paris the next day: "17,000 years old. Think of it! Imagine what humans were like back then."

Hermine brought in a platter of crisp potatoes sautéed in duck fat. Her clothes and aprons dropped for me, leaving her ivory-skinned and black haired, her nipples startlingly brown.

Across the table, two of the littlest cousins began to squirm; Marika took the youngest on her lap and played a finger game to quiet him. I watched her. I looked for some alteration. She seemed beautiful and unchanged.

The teenagers were bubbling with their usual half-suppressed laughter and sly looks. Granny sliced the large walnut tart.

I didn't go on the cave expedition. I had found out that Marika was staying home. I made some excuse which was all too readily accepted. At breakfast I dawdled, so as not to appear as hurried and furtive as I felt. Then I went off alone and hid by the river, waiting.

My parents' marriage was breaking up and that was our last family visit to the Dordogne. But all through that summer Marika and I were faithful to the river. Each day she placed her bundles by the water, pulled up her skirts and edged out onto the willow branches. Then she bathed her mysteries in the stream. I was always in an agony of being discovered, yet even when Clio came along and pointed the whole time at my hiding place Marika didn't seem to want to hunt down whatever was upsetting the dog. Sometimes I told myself that she knew I was there and welcomed it, but I was never sure, and never dared break my cover.

Always, after she left, I would strip naked and swim in the shallow pool. Each day I tried a slightly different position, each day I told myself I had seen more than the day before, but whatever wasn't gold was deepest shadow and I never felt I saw enough.

Backlighting

CASS RECLINES, NAKED, ON THE BED IN THE CORNER. HER left arm is in front of her on the sheepskin rug which covers the bed, her right arm lies along her right hip and thigh. Her legs are together, bent slightly. A screen of woven rushes covers the lower half of the window opposite her, obscuring the interior of her aunt Marika's apartment from the passers-by whose footsteps echo in the narrow Paris street.

"There's no point in doing it with clothes," Marika told her as they were washing up after lunch. "But of course, if it embarrasses you, my big American baby,"—she pinched Cass's cheek in the emphatic way the French reserve for tormenting babies in perambulators—"then we don't have to do it at all." Without a word Cass disrobed, leaving her clothes on the floor. Marika gestured to the sheepskin covered bed. Then came the question of what should be exposed. Cass, while not uncomfortable with her nakedness, had instinctively crossed her legs as she settled back onto the bed.

"Ah, no," Marika said. "You Americans are so proprietary about your bodies. Spread your legs, my dear; don't hide what you have. Bend the knee and put the foot flat on the bed, like so. Good. Now try the hand on the knee. No, no. Drape the hand on the knee." Marika stepped back and tilted her head. "Actually, no. Sometimes more is too much. We shall prefer some mystery: close the legs, bend them slightly. So. The line is more sinuous."

As Marika looks at her, now, closing one eye and cocking her head a bit, Cass feels more than naked. She puzzles over what Marika is trying to capture or accomplish with this portrait. To comfort herself she pictures her aunt at the center of some dark ritual, religious or gynecological. Marika turns back to her canvas, humming a melody Cass does not recognize. Marika is tall and heavy breasted; she has wild red hair which frizzes and curls in all directions and she wears a long blue denim dress despite the warmth of the May afternoon.

Even propped against pillows, Cass finds it hard to sit still. She wonders if she has slanted or slid down, or if her gaze has gotten somehow skewed. Each of her limbs tells her, This is not where I want to be. She tries to roll her eyes to look at the clock over Marika's desk, but she can't see it without breaking her pose. All she can see of herself is her left hand and forearm. Her arms are pins and needles; her legs may belong to someone else; her buttocks ache.

Although she has an older brother who lives in Paris, Cass chooses to stay with her aunt until she finds an apartment of her own. She is on a fellowship to study Physics for the year before graduate school. Her classes will not begin until Autumn; she has come early to get to know the city over the summer. The occasional seminars she attends, at the École Normale and the College de France, are at the limit of her understanding of both Physics and French—perhaps beyond.

Marika is the younger sister of Cass's mother; Cass always thinks of her as a "distant sister" of her mother's, the way one has "distant cousins," even though the two women had the same parents. Although she has had French citizenship for decades, Marika still surrounds herself with things Polish, carved wooden objects and elaborate cut-outs of colored paper decorate the walls; all her friends are from Eastern Europe. Occasionally she will admit that she is Jewish, but adds, "That is over now. I have paid my dues. I do not need to be Jewish any more." During the war, Cass's mother and Marika were sent from Poland to southern France where they were hidden by friends of the family. Directly afterwards Marika made her way to Paris; she has never been to America. Although Cass knew Marika from summer visits to France when she was a child, living with her now, she finds her aunt surprisingly and intractably foreign.

The walls of the front room, which serves as a studio despite its western exposure, are covered with Marika's canvases, nudes surrounded by highly patterned backgrounds. Cass is pleased by how good the pictures are and is surprised that her mother has always been so off-handed about Marika's painting. The nudes show balance, poise, equanimity; the colors are strong and wild, reminding Cass of some of the Matisses in the museum in Boston where her mother lectures.

When Marika asked her to pose, Cass was flattered; she also felt it was a way of repaying her aunt for her room and board, though she finally has a list of several possible apartments and does not think she will be staying there much longer.

Marika frowns now. Cass wonders if she has tilted out of position or if some part of her body has been recognized as misshapen or wrong. She finds she can stiffen the muscles of her toes, feet and legs, without appearing to move, if she keeps the tension equal on all sides. She can also flex arms and neck this way, but it is harder with the face. Marika is humming again, under her breath, and is dabbing a long-handled brush at her palette when the doorbell rings.

"Ah, that must be Zosha," Marika says, brightening. "Don't move, my darling. I want her to see what we are doing." Cass has been in France for two weeks and she still hasn't met any French people. Even in the Physics seminars she hasn't really talked to any of the other students. She's waiting until she feels more comfortable, perhaps in the fall.

After Marika goes to the door Cass turns her head to look but an easel blocks her view; she can hear shopping bags rustle as the two women embrace.

"Come, Zosha, come in and see my American beauty and we shall let you put on some music—your choice—and you shall make us some coffee—do not move, Cass, just a while longer. I need to finish the light on this breast." Zosha puts down her bundles and steps among the easels, her high heels clicking on the floor. Her perfume, a many-stranded scent of smoke and spice, mixes well with the smell of turpentine and linseed oil.

Marika says, "They feed them with nothing but ice cream and hamburgers, there. Everything from such fat happy cows. And still she looks like this. Can you understand it, all that golden hair? It has hints of my kind of red, I think." She touches her own hair for a moment.

Cass is not used to being inspected and discussed by Polish ladies. She resists her impulse to get up and put on her clothes only because she doesn't want Marika to know she is bothered. Presumptuous bitches, she thinks, old bags of European lard; what do you know of Physics, or anything? She is annoyed at herself for not asking Marika if she could study while posing. She could have spent this time reading about percolation theory. Instead, her body feels like an uncontrollable mound of clay. She has lost track of direction. Perhaps she is slowly rotating.

Zosha comes near, holding out her hand. "How do you do, my dear," she says. Cass shakes hands, then uses the opportunity to stretch her arms. Zosha is small, powdered, with a controlled waist, dressed in brown with a yellow scarf, long dark hair in a coil on top. Her handbag is a leather satchel, old and scraped, with an elegant clasp. Cass looks at these details rather than Zosha's face, finding it hard to look into the eyes of someone clothed when she is not.

"I am so pleased to finally make your acquaintance," says Zosha. "And what do you think of our Paris: city of love, of rational thought, science, and gastronomy?"

"Ah," says Cass, smiling and stalling. She is too proud to admit that she hasn't seen any of the love; the rational thought and science seem impenetrable; and as for gastronomy, her fellowship money allows for only the thinnest of steaks—cut, she conjectures, from stringy old horses—and french fries with the consistency of garden worms. She doesn't say this, but shrugs charmingly because she does not want to be thought surly. Still smiling, she says, "What can I say?" Seeing that Marika is frowning at her, she leans back on her pillows and looks toward the window behind her aunt.

Although this is the first time Cass has met Zosha, earlier today she had a telephone conversation with Zosha's husband.

"Who are you?" he asked.

"Cass."

"Ah." The receiver buzzed slightly. "You are the American niece." He switched to English. "I am Jacob. I am the father of at least some of the children of Marika's friend Zosha. Do you know where Zosha is?"

"No," said Cass. "I'm sorry. Marika might know, but I'm not sure when she's coming back."

"Zosha will reappear. They will both reappear." He paused. "And you my dear, how old are you?"

"How old?" said Cass, suddenly uncomfortable. "Twenty-two. Why does it matter?"

"I could not help wondering. I find myself fascinated by your voice."

Cass was silent. She found his voice interesting—low and dark and coiled—but she wished he hadn't said that.

"Perhaps you would consent to have a coffee with me?"

"No, thank you." She wasn't sure why she refused; it was a way of gaining time.

"Or a drink? An ice cream?"

"Not really, no thanks."

"Would you show yourself to me? Just your face?"

"What are you talking about?"

"I would like to glimpse you. What if I walk by Marika's apartment in ten minutes—I am not far away—would you draw back the screen and sit by the window?"

Cass found this request upsetting, that it should become so important suddenly for a stranger to see her. She didn't owe him anything, even if his voice was interesting. "No," she said, finally. "I won't come to the window and let you see me."

"You don't have to come to the window, then. You could simply pull back the screen and stay at the far end of the room. I would only be able to see your most shadowy form."

"That would be absurd," she said. "I'm afraid it's not possible. Good-bye."

Zosha goes over to the stereo system and puts on a record of Chopin Preludes; then there is the sound of coffee being ground. Cass hopes Marika will give her a coffee break. She wonders if Zosha knows about the type of requests her husband makes. She thinks more about coffee. In the study of percolation, it's a question of when the boiling water will slip between the coffee grounds, and when it won't because the grind is too fine a powder, forming a silty impenetrable mud. Then the water just sits on top. Afraid of seeming spoiled, Cass is reluctant to ask for a coffee. Marika has given so much, has let her stay so many nights, has fed her so many meals. Percolation is also when the hairbrush or comb makes it through the strands. Loose snarls—and the comb can get through; tight ones, or too many—and the hairs will break before the teeth will pass. Marika insisted on Cass brushing her hair before she posed, telling her to do it upside down until her reddish blond mane stood out in all directions, then making her stop. "Let us leave it—so," she said. "It will settle on its own. It will light the room for us."

Cass finds herself bewildered by simple problems of human relationships. Such as whether Marika likes her or not. She knows she may be too simplistic, but she cannot figure out or reconcile any two consecutive statements or actions of her aunt. Would you paint someone you couldn't stand? Would you talk the way Marika talked to Zosha about someone you love? When Cass was ten years old she had spent a summer following Marika about, ferociously captivated. Now Marika seems alien and incomprehensible.

As Cass tries to calculate how much longer the light will last, a man's voice calls from the street. "Hey-oh, Marika! Are you home? Am I very late?"

Still holding her paintbrush, Marika strides to the window, peers over the top of the woven screen and says, "Ah. Stasek. I was wondering if you had forgotten. Why don't you come in."

Cass recognizes that she and Marika are in some kind of a contest, which she can win only by continuing to recline there, no matter who comes to visit. She stays in place, wiggling her toes and fingers, hoping she will not start to blush. Stasek greets Marika at the door, murmuring, "How are you, my dear. I hope I am not late."

Cass presumes they kiss—everyone does here—but she can't hear it. Stasek comes in. His leather soled shoes tap softly as he threads his way between the easels, the paint boxes balanced on stools, the palette on the little table.

Stasek takes Cass's hand and bends to kiss it, saying, "So very pleased to meet the American niece."

Cass is startled by the touch of his lips and beard on the back of her hand. Somehow she never expected hand kissing to feel so involved and intimate. She is surprised that it would be allowed in public.

Stasek steps back and stands beside Marika, looking from Cass to the painting and back again. Cass decides, now, to stare back at him. Nothing will be gained by being embarrassed. She feels as though she is being held in a vise of air and this helps her keep her gaze steady. Stasek has a slightly grizzled beard; she saw when he bent over her hand that his eyes are green; they are also smiling and intelligent. Now his face is in shadow. The atmosphere in the room has changed: it is more crowded, and there is a slight fluttering in the air as Marika looks to Stasek for approval. Cass is surprised at this, as Marika has rarely mentioned Stasek. Now Marika's body seems to bend toward him as he walks about, and she turns to look at him almost as much as she looks at Cass.

"What do you think of the light on the legs?" Marika asks Stasek, adding, "They are not very long, but how golden she is, no? Even in the fur." She points with the handle of her brush to different parts of the canvas asking his opinion and before he can reply, says, "What about some wine?" Then, raising her voice to call above the music, "Zosha, dear, could you be an angel and bring us a couple of glasses of red?"

Zosha calls something from the kitchen. There are smells, now, of onions and Polish sausage, frying.

Stasek takes a rush-seated chair from near the window and carries it above his head as he makes his way among the easels and tables. He places his chair next to the bed, so that he is sitting beside Cass and, like her, facing Marika.

"Am I OK here?" he asks Marika. "Not in your way?"

"Not a bit."

Softly, bending toward her, he asks Cass, "What about for you, is this all right?"

"Yes," she says, speaking quietly, under the music. "It's better like that, when you are looking into the light with me."

"I thought it might be." He pauses, watching Marika. "You know," he says, privately. "You are in a position of power, like that."

"Naked?"

"In a room full of people with clothes. After all, if any of us began to strip—it would be ridiculous, it would be certifiable, we would be carted away. As the French are so fond of saying, we would be in a highly irregular position."

Cass struggles to suppress a grin. Abusing her position, she asks quietly, "Are you sleeping with Zosha?"

Stasek looks straight ahead and smiles, but before he can answer, the doorbell rings. Turning her head, Cass sees Madame Boranyi from upstairs, her bulk wrapped in a flowered housecoat; she wheezes a bit as she greets Marika. Her two granddaughters, twelve and fourteen years old, dark eyed and heavy browed, stand behind her. Madame Boranyi has an improbable tale of missing laces for hiking boots, her son is coming to visit, to retrieve his daughters, she was dusting the wardrobe and noticed that his old boots were missing laces, does Marika have any?

"Come in, my friend. I will look to see if I have any laces. Meanwhile you must come and say hello to my niece."

Cass stays where she is. Madame Boranyi visits often, sometimes several times a day if there is something on her antique mind. She has certainly seen Marika painting "from life" before.

While the young girls linger out of sight, Madame Boranyi shuffles between the easels and beside the painting tables and insists on shaking hands with Cass. Before either woman can say anything, Marika, who has been opening and closing drawers, finds some laces. "But you must stay and take some coffee with us," Marika says. "Did you know, Cass, that Madame Boranyi is from Hungary? Budapest. Her husband is Rumanian, but she prefers to keep the Hungarian name."

Cass smiles politely. Marika has already told her about her neighbor's lack of name change, several times—perhaps each time the old lady has visited. Cass cannot help thinking, Well, bully for her; I am Bostonian; perhaps I should keep my Massachusetts name if I ever marry someone from Rhode Island. She asks herself where the French people are hiding, why they never seem to come to this street, those people without a K or a Z in their name.

Marika says to Madame Boranyi, "Zosha is brewing coffee, then I am allowing her to make dinner while I just finish up this one thing while the light lasts. Please look at this hip, here: do you not think it is too abrupt?" She turns to Cass, "If you would just put your chin down one centimeter... there, one little moment more. Madame Boranyi, wouldn't you like a little wine before our coffee?"

"Ah, well, yes I would, in fact. Why this is almost like a *vernissage*, a gallery opening," murmurs Madame Boranyi. "Perhaps I should bring some little crackers?"

"You'll find some in the kitchen," says Marika. She leans forward to inspect something on the canvas, muttering, "Perhaps that is too purple, there?" then steps back to look at Stasek and once again at Cass.

"One more minute," Marika says to Cass. "Let me just find my viridian."

Zosha comes from the kitchen with a tray of glasses filled with red wine. She places one on Marika's painting table, gives one to Madame Boranyi, one to Stasek. Then she turns the record over and tells the young girls to come to the kitchen where she will give them some fruit juice.

Under cover of the music, Stasek says, "In answer to your earlier question, No. Her skin does not attract me."

"Zosha's? What's the matter with it?"

"Nothing's wrong with it; it just doesn't speak to me."

"Ah. Will I ever understand that?"

"Sooner or later, depending."

"What do you know about Zosha and Jacob?"

"Why?"

Cass describes Jacob's phone call.

He laughs, "And you wouldn't do it?" He looks at her and holds his wine glass to her lips. She gulps furtively, hoping Marika won't notice.

"Thanks. No, I don't know why. I liked his voice, but there was something in the situation I couldn't meet. He wanted it so much: just to see me, he said. If that was all he wanted, it sounded sick, and if it wasn't all he wanted, well, I wasn't interested. Maybe it was the imbalance of desire. Am I making any sense? Are you sleeping with Marika, then?"

Stasek leans toward Cass, again giving her a taste of his wine. He says, "You are perfectly clear. Yes, actually, I have recently become involved with your aunt."

Marika whistles to Stasek from her easel, then blows him a kiss. "Could you move back a little, Stasek; you do strange things to the light if you lean too far forward. Zosha, dear, could we have the rest of that wine? And perhaps the coffee if it is ready. Crackers, cookies—somehow I am starving. See if Madame Boranyi's girls need some cookies, no?"

"I can hear the girls," Cass says to Stasek. "But I can't see them, sitting like this. What are they up to?"

"In the kitchen, eating cookies and orange juice with Zosha. Before, they stood in the doorway playing some sort of jumping game with elastic. They kept their faces turned away from you; your nakedness made them uneasy, I think."

"But they have met me before," says Cass.

"I think, at that tender age, one prefers things wrapped up."

"Does it attract you, that age?"

"Few ages don't."

"As long as the skin…?"

"Correct."

"Are you monogamous?"

"Not terribly. Life is very short."

"What do you do," she asks.

"In life, or with those who attract me?"

Cass smiles, then remembers the expression Marika wants from her, a kind of straightforward, observant, all-powerful gaze. "In life, I meant."

"Wondrous photographs and lesser poems; I am working to reverse it."

Cass can see that the long afternoon light is still warm and yellow on the skin of her arm and hand and she knows that her face and Stasek's are full of that light. She suspects, though, that Marika is painting her in streaks of greens and purples, like some wild animal in a perverse nocturnal forest.

As the late golden sun slants through the top of the window, it shines through Marika's red hair in a sizzling fringe; it blackens the easels into gaunt unlikely structures; it glints off the top of Zosha's black chignon and through her yellow scarf; it turns Madame Boranyi into a small dark rock, making the rims of her ears glow pink, and fans her granddaughters' dresses into white billowing sails. Cass looks out at the room serenely.

Shadows

FOUR IN THE MORNING. ANCIENT SPIRALS AND COILS GLIDE over the ceiling, shadows of the balcony cast by the head-lights of a car in the Rue du Cherche-Midi several floors below. Marion, at fierce odds with her eighty-four year old body, watches from her bed. As always, car and shadows move in opposite directions.

Nocturnal lucidity: her mind glows at this hour, recalls her old friends who are gone or dying. She has grieved as they dwindled into fragile husks and then lingered, too long, in a state that was neither living nor dead. Yesterday she kept watch over a colleague who, decades earlier, had been her lover. The hospital room was dim; in hushed tones, the nuns in their dark habits told her what to watch for—Speak to him, they said, Hearing is the last sense to go. Marion sat with him, clasping his pale hand in hers, and spoke quietly of caves they had explored together, not knowing if her words penetrated his stillness, his occasional breaths being the only movements he could make. She sat and whispered until all color and motion departed.

⌒

Across the ceiling plays another beam of light. The tendrilled ironwork of the balcony rises up and slides backwards, then stops, stretches out of shape, and turns around, as though searching for something. Tracking it, Marion wonders briefly if it is looking for her; she shifts her head too quickly—a sharp pinch in her neck. Rubbing the back of her head, she decides that nothing decrees that she stay in bed until just before the bakery opens. At six-thirty she will be there as usual—greeting her old acquaintance, Tournivelle, the astronomer—but she doesn't have to lie in bed until then. She is old enough to decide anew.

She rolls to her side and pushes herself up on a diagonal, then edges her legs off the bed and inches her feet into felt slippers. Her pulse feels erratic. Remembering her dying friend's limp hands, she clenches her fists, spreads her fingers wide, then half closes them into claws. She repeats this until her hands start to ache, then works her legs, flexing her feet until the strings along the back of her legs are tight, finally pointing her toes until the tops of her calves prickle and come alive. She circles her feet in one direction then the other until she can believe in her ankles.

Marion hears the hissing of the street-cleaning truck down below. Those cleaners keep good hours and she is fond of them. She is old and her bones creak.

Even though it is August and the night is warm, Marion wants some hot apple soup, a dish she finds very soothing. Raising one hand to her head, she splays her fingers and ruffles her wiry gray hair until it is no longer matted from lying down. She ties her dove-colored silk dressing gown around her and goes to the kitchen where she peels and cuts a pair of apples and cooks them in an iron pot with water and a dash of cinnamon. From time to time she taps the handle of the wooden spoon against the rim of the pot.

Carrying her soup to the table by the living room window, she opens the lace curtains, then sits in the tall-backed chair. The sweeping truck has passed; she can hear it turning the corner and lowering its brushes. Eating slow spoonfuls, she watches the street.

The cobblestones are still glistening from being sprayed and swept. A white cat on a nighttime mission shies and skitters as a manhole cover in the middle of the sidewalk lifts then moves to the side with a dull clang. A young man peers from the hole, looking cautiously around him. Flinging his knapsack onto the pavement, he climbs out and shoves the heavy iron disk back in place.

Pulling her robe tighter, Marion gets up, opens the tall windows and walks out onto the balcony. It is the third time she has seen this curly-haired boy emerge on her sidewalk in the middle of the night. She smiles. She knows the attractions of exploring underground. Though the caverns she has worked on are older, more connected with ancient things, she understands the urge to be underneath the city while it hums and sleeps: the secret silent descents through unused railroad tunnels, the long expeditions, then the ascents—miles away—perhaps astonishing late night revelers, perhaps tumbling into the arms of the police, who consider these clandestine explorations outside the law.

"*Bonsoir*," Marion calls down to him through the night silence.

The boy looks up, startled. "*Bonsoir Madame*," he calls, his voice echoing slightly against the stones. "It's just explorations; please don't call the police." His French is correct but the American accent unmistakable. Marion has lost her own accent long ago.

"Do not insult me," she calls down to him in English, leaning forward over the railing.

"Sorry—it's just that a lot of old people don't like to see us coming up out of the street, and then they call the cops and it's a lot of bother."

"Probably jealous, you know. We are stuck above." She pauses, then says, "You must be hungry. Why don't you come up for some bread and cheese, or a cognac?"

"I'm filthy. I've been down all night."

"I can spread newspapers. Hold on, I'll buzz the street door for you. Take the elevator if you are tired. It's the *troisième à gauche*, the name is Forrest."

While the boy makes his way in, Marion goes to the massive carved wardrobe in her bedroom for a sheet to spread over the living room couch; it will be easier to take the sheet to the laundry than to get rock dust out of the velvet cushions. It is not like her to invite in this pre-dawn stranger, but she is tired of old habits. Yesterday, in the hospital, before her friend's hands went limp they had become suddenly bloated and plump, like fishes.

Although most of her old colleagues are gone, she does not like the younger ones: their ambition makes them fawn over her and she does not trust their anxious friendship or their constant questions about her unpublished papers. She has no desire to show her archives to them. Long retired from her position at the museum, she still sits each day alone at her desk, revising her writings, making order out of her files of photographs, maps and drawings of the caves which she and her crew discovered and documented when she was younger. As she works, she looks up from her notes and sighs, trying to get rid of the feeling that a boulder presses down on her, crushing her ribs. She wonders if it is grief or the dwindling process.

Marion lays a trail of newspapers from the kitchen to the front hall. When she opens the door the boy is standing there, his hair a mass of honey-colored tangles, his cheeks still flushed from his explorations. His black jumpsuit is streaked with limestone dust. Marion gestures to his boots, and he says, "Oh. I'm sorry," and bends down to take them off. Standing up again, he puts out his hand. "My name is Tenso. At least that's what I'm called down there."

Marion looks at his hand, crusted with dirt, but does not shake it. She nods, smiling. Half a century earlier her colleagues who frequented the catacombs under Paris used pseudonyms when they were below ground. She says, "You can wash up in there if you like," gesturing toward the kitchen sink. She sniffs the air: the boy has a faint smell of chalk dust about him.

While he is washing, Marion makes another path of newspapers from the kitchen to the living room. Tenso steps care-

fully along several days' worth of *Le Monde*, and settles into
the sheet-covered sofa; he watches as she pads in her slippers
to the liquor cabinet. She pours two snifters of brandy and
hands one to him. He drinks without pausing to swirl it about
and inhale it, then grins and says, "Do you really have some
bread and things?"

"Go and look in the kitchen; you will find cheese inside
the fridge; the bread is on top." She is pleased at the idea of
his visit, but she is not about to wait on him. "Take what you
like," she calls.

This Tenso can't be older than twenty-one or -two, she
thinks. She is struck by his unusual tawny beauty. Although
she does not really like the young as a rule—their smooth
skins lack history and their eyes make her think of barnyard
animals—she admires the frankness with which they show
their dislike of old age. It is people between twenty-nine and
sixty-five who are awful, she has observed: they have a smug-
ness to them—mixed with terror as they get older—leading
them to straighten up in her presence, as though their bodies
are saying, You see, I can still stand tall and still suck in my
gut.

Marion asks Tenso about his expedition this night and
he explains that he has moved into the neighborhood only a
month earlier. An engineering student in the States, he is
taking a year off from school. He loves bridges and tunnels,
elegant solutions to problems of span and support, but, he
says, his obsession is subterranean Paris. He has been exploring the region beneath this neighborhood. Tonight he descended at midnight, near Alésia, and walked through the
systems of the 14th and the 6th *arrondissements*.

As he tries to describe the flavor of the tunnels Marion interrupts. "I have lived here for almost sixty years," she says. "My friends used to go down on the right bank, underneath the sixteenth *arrondissement*. When I was finishing my doctorate in the *Musée de l'Homme*, the anthropology museum at Trocadéro, you could still get into the tunnels from the basement. They would invite me to come with them, but I always refused. For me it was the caves of the Dordogne, with their paintings and carvings which took over my mind and my life. The mysteries." She stands and steps carefully to the liquor cabinet. After pouring more cognac for the boy, she places the bottle near her on the coffee table. Sitting again, she taps her fingers on the arms of her chair as she watches him. "After my studies came more field work. I worked on paintings, drawing and photographing them—you may have seen my books. But I also worked on prehistoric music."

"How on earth can you know anything about their music?" Tenso asks.

"This, of course, is harder—more speculative. But they always had music in the caves. They made flutes from hollowed leg bones of sheep and birds, adding whistle-heads to one end, like a recorder, to make the sound sweeter. They had bull-roarers made from ivory, and we're sure they had percussion instruments, though we tend not to find drums: hides don't last, wood doesn't last—under normal conditions."

"So what do you have?"

"We have evidence—this was my work, actually—that they used stalactites and stalagmites as musical instruments. Only certain formations, the ones which look like folded drapery. They decorated the folds with painted symbols and also broke them off at different heights; this varies the pitch. Then when you hit them with bones or sticks it can sound like gongs or harps or drums, depending on which cave you are in, and how you strike them. Anyway, finally I was offered a position at the museum. I never went back to America, except for short visits. The caves, and the men I loved, they were all here in France." She refills her own glass and holds it up to the light, wondering what it would be like to teach this boy something about prehistory, to divert him from his subterranean Paris to the wilder regions of southern France.

Tenso turns to the plate of cheese he has brought from the kitchen. He has ripped the bread into chunks. The Brie is congealed into an agate-like translucent mass. He cuts it thinly and pops the slices into his mouth.

"I wish the cheese were less decrepit for you," Marion says. She is pleased that he does not seem shocked by her inviting him up. Instead, he seems to feel at home, as though this visit were a simple extension of his earlier prowls; she feels comfortable telling him about her work.

"Do you still go into any caves?" he asks, spreading his bread with crumbling goat cheese.

"I haven't been to the south in years. The surface caves do not really interest me, the deep ones are simply too strenuous for me, at present." She finds it hard to admit this aloud.

"Why do you old people stop exercising, anyway?" Tenso bursts out. "Manhole covers, you know, weigh at least a hundred pounds. Then there are rungs in the wall you have to climb, sixty feet or so, straight up or down. Sit-ups," he says. "Push-ups; chin-ups. That would do it." He inhales, as though in preparation.

"Ah," she says. "Well. But you know, even if I were strong enough, it is not under *Paris* I would be exploring." Rubbing away drops of cognac he has spilled on the table, she says, "Few of the tunnels under this city are very old." She tells him what he already knows, of the quarries and subterranean inspection tunnels which honeycomb present-day Paris. "While the paintings in the caves I have always been interested in," she says, "date from at least 15,000 years ago."

"Yeah. OK. But why does that matter?"

"It matters because distant time is so hard for us to conceive. The Gauls are shadowy to us, even Caesar seems infinitely distant. But down in the caves you come upon an intelligence, an eye for observing and painting that feels suddenly closely related to us. You feel that they understood the essence of creation; how to invoke its wildness and then how to render it. You can see this in their paintings and sculpture, and my guess is that their music showed the same combination of understanding, mastery, and wildness. This is what has driven my life. Down there everything seems totally clear and completely mysterious at the same time." She pauses, hoping she has not gone too far. "Now the work of your catacombs and quarries," she says. "Is it not, at best, good masonry? And at worst simply functional, 'technical tunnels' for electric wires and telephone lines? I know the catacombs aren't the same as the sewers, but they might as well be, no?"

"No, not at all." Tenso throws his hands up in contradiction. Marion is pleased by this; none of her young colleagues favor her with open disagreement: she is too old, too eminent.

"You're completely wrong," Tenso says. Leaning down,

he rubs his calves as though to keep them from cramping, stretches his legs in front of him, then gets up suddenly and begins to pace about in his stocking feet. "The thing of it is," he says, finally. "The thing about the catacombs—it's not the architecture, not that, though that's often fascinating and strange. It's not even that I can go down there at midnight and walk the system and see in the distance the glow of another carbide lamp and know that there is someone for me to talk to." He pauses. "It's something else that overcomes you and it's hard to put into words." He stops pacing and turns toward her, suddenly. "You should see it, you know."

"Ah" she says. "If only I could." It is her turn to be annoyed, slightly; she feels teased by his suggestion and its implied refusal to take her body, her age, into account. Peevishly, she says, "Even stairs—you know—I have some trouble climbing them." She does not mention her pulse. She tries to tell him about the paintings in the caves, the ochre flanks of horses, the haunches of charcoal bulls. "Some of the cattle are now extinct," she says. "Take the aurochs, for example."

"Wait," says Tenso. "Let's leave the question of antique livestock for the moment. We'll return to it some other time. Listen. What about *us* making a descent here in Paris?"

"How do you mean?"

"We'll have dinner down there. We often do that, you know. We'll bring wine."

Marion looks at him quizzically; she flexes her hands. Then, no longer petulant, she asks, "What is it, sixty feet down? A hundred?" She pauses. "How would I get down there?" She smiles. "How would I get out again?" Her heartbeat takes off in an odd patter.

"I have friends. We'll lower you. And bring you up again."

To keep from showing how excited she is, Marion gives a bitter laugh. "When I feel like being reduced to a sack of potatoes, I will be sure to call you."

"Reduced?" Tenso whispers, as though he feels he can say any truth if he says it soft enough. "Is staying up here all the time what you really want?" He makes a sweeping gesture which seems to include Marion, her cognac, her velvety apartment. Then, as if wondering if he is being too savage, he gives a collusive wink and smiles as he approaches her. "It's August, remember." He touches the arm of her chair and leans toward her. "The Parisians are gone. The *gendarmes* who patrol down there have gone off on vacation; even the ones who wait in their unmarked cars by our favorite exits are gone." He springs away again, saying, "They've taken *maman* and all the little chickies to their bungalows by the sea shore." He comes toward her again, smiling, almost prancing. He looks her up and down, as though measuring her for an engineering problem. "You don't weigh very much. We could manage; we could really bring it off. We've been needing something like this, something like you. You could tell us things. I mean, we know the systems under Paris and the suburbs, but we really don't know anywhere else." Tenso goes back to the couch. "Oh God," he sighs almost to himself. "It feels good to lie down. If I fell asleep here, would you mind?"

Marion doesn't answer. Her hand touches the neckline of her dressing gown and smoothes it, making sure it has not come open.

Turning to face her he says, "We'll rig up something. I'll take good care of you. A feather-soft descent. Tell me: aren't you tempted? By the way, I may be falling asleep."

Marion holds up her hands to make him stop. She is flattered by his attention and by his ability to talk to her. As she looks at his wiry body, she considers why he would want to go to all the trouble. It could be feelings of kinship for other subterranean travelers, but it is equally likely that he is tickled by the purely mechanical problems of getting her down into the catacombs. He may also want to show her off to his friends. She does not care what his reasons are; her own need is so imperative. She feels such a wild panic that she suddenly has to get out of his presence for a moment. "I shall go and wash," she says abruptly. "You stay and rest."

In her own bedroom, Marion pulls back the heavy curtain to let in the dawn. She lowers herself into the chair at her dressing table. That face. She hasn't gotten used to this old skin with its creases and wrinkles running at cross-purposes. It still has a certain strength, though, and when the light is right, its old beauty shows.

To prepare her face for the morning, she slathers on cream and massages it upwards, then goes over it with small resounding slaps. She tissues off the extra cream and slaps some more. She powders, dabs her eyelids with blue, and streaks a black pencil across the upper lid. Crimson on her lips, then powder to keep the red from seeping, then more crimson on top for color. Finally she smiles at her image and gets up deliberately. Entering the living room, she sits down and says, "Listen to me."

Tenso wakes and turns to look at her.

Marion speaks slowly to contain her excitement. "I would be thrilled to come down with you; it is what I have been looking for." She leans back and closes her eyes for a moment, visualizing the unholy exertion of it all. Then she watches Tenso's face. Trying to keep any hint of desperation from her voice, she adds, "There's also the question of food. Of course I will pay for our dinners down there, for your friends as well. I will also keep fresh food supplies here for you. You can tell me what you need." Not waiting for him to reply, she stands, straightening her back with precise attention.

By six-thirty, Marion is at the bakery, watching Madame Clement, the baker's wife, drag the red leatherette chair to the front and climb up on it to reach the brass lock at the top of the glass door. This morning Marion is first in a line of two. She feels a sense of urgency; or perhaps it is hunger. She grins and turns to her competitor, the old astronomer. "Aha, Tournivelle. Too old to get up early, are you. You've got to be quick in this life to get anywhere."

"Most dear Lady," replies the professor, insisting on using his form of English. "Your triumphs are sandwiched by your losses. Yesterday, for example, and, if I may argue by induction, tomorrow. What will you buy this morning? A little something to go with your peanut butter?" Tournivelle accuses Marion each morning at the bakery of being an "eater of peanut-butter." She knows it is his way of teasing her for her American birth and upbringing, though she does not, in fact, eat peanut butter any longer, being somewhat afraid of getting locked in her own mouth. She has not been back to California in forty years. She never felt at home in all that sun. Unlike the rest of her family, she was never blond or muscular. Her skin would never tan. When she was a child, if friends or family prevailed on her to come to the beach, she would gravitate to the shade of an overhanging rock and stay there fully clothed, her eyes protected by sunglasses with round black lenses. Her two older brothers called her "The Owl."

Marion asks for her usual butter croissant and baguette, then doubles her order on account of Tenso. She is filled with a sudden energy and a desire for more company; she wants to break her pattern with Tournivelle of ironic and cheerful salutations at the bakery doorstep. Today, as she puts her change into her coin purse and he starts to tip his hat to her, she says, "I will wait for you outside; I would like to ask you something." She stands just outside the door, knowing this will frustrate Madame Clement who prides herself on her hearing.

Tournivelle pushes open the glass bakery door, clutching his breads. "Fine morning, Marion. A bit gray?" As she nods agreement, she wonders if he is referring to her or the day. No matter, they both are. All three of them, rather: man, woman, and sky. The sky is opalescent, the air smells of flint.

"What I wanted to know," she stops and clears her throat in a small growl. "Was whether you wouldn't like to take breakfast with me. I have plenty of coffee. There is an elevator, and today it is working."

Tournivelle looks pleased and surprised. "Usually," he says, "I hate to be with anyone at breakfast, but your invitation flatters me. If you let me go home and read my papers afterwards, I will come with you now."

As Marion and Tournivelle get out of the iron grillwork elevator and she hunts in her handbag for her keys, she watches Tournivelle inspect the chalky footprints leading to her door. She wonders if that was part of her reason for inviting him to breakfast, to show off the fact that she already has a visitor. She opens the door.

"Have you a new dog, then?" Tournivelle asks. He places his hat on the brass hook by the door, then steps beside the trail of newspapers and sniffs the air.

"No, no," she laughs, then whispers, "I have a young visitor." She searches in the living room and out on the balcony. "Ah, well, he seems to have gone home." She tries to keep the disappointment from her voice as she shows Tournivelle the crumpled sheet on the couch. She decides not to tell much about Tenso's visit, yet. The whole morning has been so odd that she is still delighted as she seats Tournivelle at her dining room table and surrounds him with small porcelain plates and coffee cups.

Some days later, Tenso rings Marion's bell at midnight. His black jumpsuit is clean, his hair shines in the yellow light of the corridor.

"Are you set, then?" he asks. "I won't come in, if you're

all ready."

They take the elevator to the ground floor. A dark green van is waiting for them, its motor echoing in the quiet street. Tenso introduces Marion to his friends sitting in the back seat: "*La Taupe*," he says. "The Mole." A thin girl with light brown hair cut into bangs gives Marion a shy smile and extends her hand. Marion is surprised by the strength of the girl's fingers.

"And this is Monsieur James."

Mr. James, a fleshy, bearded young man dressed completely in brown reaches over and clasps Marion's bony hand in both of his thick ones. "I am so very pleased you could come with us tonight," he says, proudly, in a formal highly-accented English.

Marion thanks him and tells them all they can speak French if they prefer.

Tenso stops the van near the fence of the Parc Montsouris in the 14th *arrondissement*. "This park is wonderfully 'permeable' at night," he says. "But I guess we should still be rather quiet. Taupe, if you could just escort Madame to the bushes, she can wait while we get things ready."

Marion sits on a large stone surrounded by shrubs. Behind her is the children's playground. The night is clear. The moon has not yet risen but the stars, increasingly rare over Paris, seem unusually many and active. Clanking noises come from the van where the young people are unloading.

Taupe pulls at an iron leaf grating until she has lifted it from a round opening in the grass. Flicking on the miner's light on her forehead, she disappears into the ground carrying a knapsack. Tenso and James then begin rigging a tripod over the same hole, attaching ropes and a pulley. When they hear a soft whistle from down below, they lower a wheeled contraption and two more knapsacks.

Marion is happy sitting on the boulder; she is a bit warm as she has piled many layers of clothing under her old slate-colored canvas caving suit, knowing it might be chilly down below and that extra padding can be welcome in stone passages. Her helmet seems from another era, strips of brown leather stitched together, with a strap under the chin. She has dosed herself with enough aspirin to quiet her joints against unusual twists and motions. Tenso disappears into the opening as James beckons Marion to join him at the pulley.

The descent is through an "air well." Suspended on the leather seat of the harness, Marion takes up almost all the room. James has told her to keep a hand on the iron rungs as she goes down; that way she won't bump into them. It smells of water and dirt and cement. Taupe is shining a light directly up and Marion can see the shadows of her own body on the cement walls above. Tenso, also down below, is in charge of all her ropes.

At the bottom, Taupe has set up a wheelchair so that they can get around more quickly. He helps Marion into it while they wait for James to join them.

Through the limestone tunnels: sometimes high arched ceilings, sometimes lower flat ones where the three young people have to duck their heads. Marion, being wheeled in the chair, is surprised at how smooth it is. Street names are stenciled or carved into the walls and correspond to the surface thoroughfares far above. The stone is yellow in the light from their head lamps; the breeze is cool but not cold.

Tenso turns Marion's chair down a short passageway. He stops suddenly and wheels her around so that she is facing a marble fountain. "Well," he says. "What do you think?" He is silent for a moment. "It belonged to an old abbey above here." He offers her his arm and helps her out of her wheelchair, then takes the chair cushion and sets it on the ground for her.

Taupe unfolds a striped blanket for them to sit on. She takes loaves of bread and bottles of Bordeaux from one of the knapsacks, unwraps a large Brie, then starts a spirit lamp and begins heating dinner. "I made it this morning—it's just a beef stew," she says. "But I think it's kind of a good thing to have down here."

James takes fresh candles from his pack; he secures them at intervals, standing each one in a small puddle of melted wax. He lights them and turns off the torches one by one. The glow on the stone walls is golden and dancing.

As they eat, the young men describe to Marion the changes which take place in the tunnels. "You know, it's really almost alive," says James. "Each week the city authorities block up new passages with cement. Then our people come—after a certain time has elapsed—and delicately, well, blast them open."

"Or," says Tenso, "The police decide it's time to weld shut the manholes. That takes a certain amount of prying to undo. Truck jacks work best."

After dinner they move to a small chapel carved from the rock. Taupe produces a bottle of cognac. James lights a single candle this time. Sitting down beside Marion, Tenso asks her if she's all right. "Splendid," she replies. They lean back against the wall and through her layers of clothing she can feel his body, solid like the rock.

Home at three in the morning, Marion takes more aspirin before going to bed, not because anything hurts, but because she suspects it might. She sleeps soundly for almost three hours. When she gets to the bakery Tournivelle is just leaving.

"Well, well," he says, gloating and tipping his hat. "Better late than never?"

"Ah, well."

"Why don't you join me in the gardens in the middle of the morning? We can take a stroll."

As she accepts, Marion knows that it is really an invitation to sit by him in his favorite spot by the Médici fountain; this fills her with pleasure.

It is 10:45 in the morning. Having passed through the gates of the Luxembourg Gardens, Marion stops to sit on a park bench. The morning mist has burned off and the August sun feels sharp on her face and neck; she shifts to a seat under the chestnut trees. She watches the other people in the park and sees an American girl she knows lying on a nearby bench, red hair flaming as she gives her young skin to the sun.

Soon the gravel is shimmering in the light, so Marion gets up again and walks down the path to the Médici Fountain. There the viscous black water of the reflecting pool seems, as always, to flow uphill, while at the far end the marble lovers cavort in their nakedness, oblivious to the bronze giant, Polyphemus, who spies on them from above. Tournivelle sits on a spindly metal chair by the pool, keeping an eye on a necking couple a few seats away.

"Ah, Tournivelle. Keeping busy, I see."

Tournivelle, startled, stands to greet her; he kisses her cheeks. "No trouble negotiating the crossing?"

Marion shakes her head and lowers herself to the chair from which he has whisked his hat. Through the morning their bodies weave and bob towards each other and away, as they move in their chairs toward the shade.

Sitting with Tournivelle, Marion speaks more than she has in months or years. At first she talks of caving and her early work with prehistoric painting and music in the south. Finally she tells of this past night's explorations beneath Paris.

As Marion describes her midnight penetration of the Parc Montsouris, Tournivelle slides the brim of his hat slowly through his fingers. The descent by harness makes him shift in his park chair, crossing his legs and then uncrossing them again. When she tells of the tunnels and fountains he begins to look at her as though he has trouble figuring out who she is.

"Wouldn't you like to make a descent with us?" she asks. "I'm sure my young friends would be pleased. The dinner they provide is rustic but it is well-cooked."

Tournivelle takes her hand and pats it, laughing nervously. "Ah no. No, I do not think that world is for me. Very daring of you, I must say, and very American. I am not ready for it, though. I will wait for you here at ground level and we will have breakfast together." He brings her hand to his lips.

Down in the tunnels, a week later, Marion has brought a small knapsack with her. Tenso helps her into the wheelchair; she takes from her sac a woolen blanket which he tucks around her. As Tenso pushes her chair the light from his head lamp bounces from wall to wall and occasionally shines straight ahead in the long gallery in front of them. The beige stone passage fades to a black rectangle in the distance.

Taupe and James are following behind and their lamps cast shadows of a lanky man and a seated woman. James's backpack is bulky and it gives a hollow thud when it bumps against the wall. It is quiet, except for that occasional thump, and their footsteps, and the wheels of Marion's chair, going now over packed dirt, now over stones. At one point Tenso stops, saying, "Listen." Water, somewhere out of sight, falls by single drops into an unseen pool.

Though the ceiling is still high, the passage has become narrower and the walls are covered with graffiti painted in black and red and green. Marion asks Tenso to go slowly so that she can read them, and then asks him to stop as she roots about in her sac for her cosmetics case and takes out an eyebrow pencil. "Would you help me out," she asks Tenso, pushing her blanket to the side. "I would like to leave my scrawl." Tenso offers her his arm as she walks. Choosing a clean patch of wall Marion puts her black pencil to her tongue, then writes in tall thin letters: "*Hibou.*" Night Owl.

The way broadens again and the ochre-colored stones of the walls are smaller and more irregular. Stumpy pillars stand at intervals, holding up the ceiling; in the jigging play of lights they lose their stillness. "We've gone farther tonight," says Tenso. "There's still so much to show you." He slows her chair then turns it sharply down a side gallery. Here the way twists back and forth, and at each turning the path ahead falls momentarily into darkness until Tenso's light catches up with the direction of the wheelchair.

They have entered a round hall, almost two stories high. As Taupe and James shine their lights for her, and Tenso slowly rotates her chair, Marion can see concentric rings of different rock layers at the center of the arched ceiling where, over time, progressive cave-ins have made the room higher. Lower down, niches have been carved into the walls, and in these James proceeds to place his candles, finally turning off his head lamp and motioning Tenso and Taupe to do the same. At one side of the room a low wall surrounds a pool or well; here, too, James puts his candles.

While Taupe sets out their dinner on the striped blanket, Tenso and Marion inspect the pool. Tenso plays the beam of his flashlight over the water illuminating the steps which continue down below the surface until they are lost in the murky blueness.

∞

After dinner Taupe pours cognac into their wine cups, and Marion, smiling, produces a small box of dark chocolates from her sac. They sit, drinking, eating chocolates, and smoking.

"Listen," Marion says at last. "I should like to propose something. I hope you will continue to bring me down here, although I know it is a lot of trouble." Tenso starts to protest but she silences him. "I do have something to give in return." She turns to face Tenso. "It is this: when I die—how long can I last after all?—I would like to leave you my maps and writings. Some of the caves I write about are known but not published; others are already in the literature but incompletely. I have charted the entrances to galleries and chambers which are not accessible to the casual visitor. I show the locations of the calcite formations which produce the strangest musical sounds. Somewhere I still have the old recordings of us playing sheep bone flutes accompanied by bull-roarers and drumming on stalactite gongs. Of course, if you are not interested, you can turn everything over to the Musée de l'Homme."

"Oh, but I am," Tenso says, getting up and standing in front of her.

"Then," Marion smiles. "You do what you will."

"But it isn't," Tenso hesitates. He begins pacing. "It's not why we brought you down here, to get something from you..."

"Don't worry," she says. "I know that." She finishes her cigarette and stubs it out. "That is one of the reasons I wanted to give everything to you. My colleagues will be unspeakably annoyed." She grins broadly. "They will call it frivolous. They will think I've gone mad. They will be doubly wrong. I am old enough to recognize what I want. I want you to see my world."

A bluish haze ascends slowly towards the vaulted ceiling. Marion reaches forward and picks up the chocolate box again, tapping it with her fingertips before she opens it. As though in answer to her, James gets up and blows out several of the candles, turning the room into a darker, more intimate gold. He opens his knapsack and extracts a wooden drum: its sides are incised with geometric patterns, its head covered with hide. James offers the drum to Tenso who declines by shaking his head and smiling, and to Taupe who also refuses, so he carries it to the far wall. There, sitting in the semi-darkness, he begins a soft tapping of tentative calls. Expanses of silence pulse between his refrains. Tenso sits down again beside Marion, lights a cigarette and gives it to her. Lighting another for himself, he shifts closer to her and puts his arm around her. Marion settles into his protective warmth.

As James intensifies his riffs the shadowed walls start to throb. The drumming isn't deadened by the stone. Reverberating, it hovers in the smoky haze, somewhere in the middle of the dome-shaped room; as the candles flicker with the vibrations, shadows dart and return, and the surface of the water quivers in a standing wave. The beating of the drum feeds on the walls, gaining, growing vast and thick and bellowing until there are no silences but a continuous timeless roar. The drumming becomes the water and becomes the smoke and becomes the flame until the stone itself turns into sound.

Raw Desire

I NO LONGER EAT ANYTHING COOKED," ZOSHA SAID. "ONLY RAW. Jacob also. We thought you could try it with us. How could it hurt, for one night only?"

Cass looked around the table to see how the other guests would react. No one said anything. She couldn't tell if they were used to Zosha's strange regimens, or if they were simply choosing not to show their dismay.

At each place was a hemisphere of orange melon.

"Smell," Zosha exhorted her guests. "Modern man has forgotten his nose. It is necessary to smell before you taste." Cass, obedient, inhaled the sun-baked sweetness.

The table was covered with a sea green cloth. Between carved wooden candlesticks were the platters of food: a white oval plate with dark red tomatoes; a rough-surfaced earthenware plate crossed with strips of fat; a long cobalt platter bearing halved avocados, light green and empty; a steel bowl filled with curly lettuce; a black metal tray spread with pinkish strips of raw pork; a grey ceramic jug holding a cluster of broad beans; a white plate of small dark green peppers; another white plate with green onions. These are ingredients, Cass thought, not dinner.

Cass had not come willingly. Aunt Marika, Zosha's closest friend, had insisted Cass show up, with flowers, she had added, but not chrysanthemums, which in France were used 'only for death wishes.' Cass presumed she meant funerals. She had bought a thick clutch of violets from a peasant woman standing in the shadow of Notre Dame. Smelling of far away mornings, these violets were probably incorrect in some other way.

"Well, La Science, how are you my darling?" Zosha had kissed her at the door. All these old European women grew whiskers, Cass thought, perhaps it was the minerals in the water: calcium, magnesium, you could see them listed on the sides of bottles. Zosha took the flowers with another bristly kiss and exclamations to Aunt Marika, then both of them chortling, in Polish, most likely something about the mountains, or being young and elsewhere.

Wishing she hadn't come, Cass had inspected the posters on the walls, advertising Zosha's productions of Polish theater in Paris: drab fatigued colors streaked by sharp red, a hunter's cap on a bed of mushrooms, a rainy forest surrounded by leering faces, the lettering ironic, distorted, and unreadable.

Stasek, Marika's lover, had been standing at the window, gazing at the old cathedral. He had turned to greet Cass, when she entered, taking in her cropped and curly red hair, her mustard yellow t-shirt, attractive and inappropriate, her earrings with a bit of gold wire around bone, from a street vendor, probably. He wanted to photograph her. Marika had painted her a week earlier. They all wanted to capture her, as though at twenty-two she was at some critical point. "Cass," he said, kissing her briefly and letting her go. "Come and see how Notre Dame is trapping what is left of the late spring sun."

Cass had stood with him looking out the window, trying to see beyond the ornateness of the architecture into the geometry, all quadrangles and nested triangles, trefoils and strange arches, while on the pavement its huge shadow stretched, mysterious in its simplicity. The forces intrigued her: compression here, tension there, everything thrusting. The purpose of it did not interest her. That was for others, possibly. She had tried to understand the construction; there were people who claimed to be guides to the cathedral—she had followed one of them, a strange old priest who told of losing his youth and his health in Africa—but these were no guides, really; they were explaining themselves, not the edifice. The oldness mystified her, weighed on her. Space, emptiness, smell—all crystallized by time.

Zosha had seated Cass between Stasek and Jacob, Zosha's husband. Cass wondered if there was still some way she could get out of this whole gathering, some illness or outburst which would allow her to make her to exit and slink back to Aunt Marika's place where she was living. She could hyperventilate and faint—but they would all gather around her and that would be worse. She thought of performing her seal imitation, the one where she flopped her hands vigorously in front of her face while inhaling and barking at the same time.

Next to Stasek, at the foot of the table, sat Marion, who held herself like a queen, but looked, Cass thought, like an adamant old lizard. Cass found her familiar, but could not place her, until the elderly lady leaned forward, saying, "The last time I saw you, my dear, you must have been nine or so; I'm not very good with ages. It was at your grandmother's. In the Dordogne."

"I was ten, actually," Cass said, relieved to know why Marion seemed familiar. "That was the last time I was in France."

Beside Marion sat a man in a brown suit and a well-groomed woman with thin blond hair, they seemed to be a couple and to speak neither English nor French. Cass could not remember their names; they didn't speak any language she knew. The man's hair was too black and he had liverish circles under his eyes. On his other side sat Marika. Zosha was at the head of the table, on her left an ancient whiskery Frenchman, Tournivelle, his black three-piece suit covered with fly-specks.

Cass was relieved that Stasek was next to her. The first time they had met, at Marika's, he had aligned himself with her, sitting at her side, watching the slanting light stream into the room while Marika painted her portrait. That day Cass had been able to talk with Stasek: their language had a privacy and receptivity like the embrace of a soft couch.

Now, a chattering of Polish around the table. As Cass wondered if she would understand anything the whole evening, a wave of French sizzled through and passed. Talk settled into

English.

"Relax," Stasek said softly. "All dinner parties are terrible. I'm surprised they got you to come."

"It was to please Aunt Marika," Cass said. "She lets me stay in her place, so I'm trying to behave, at least until I find a place of my own. She calls me her American baby with no stories."

Stasek examined her. How much golden skin the young had: they were all limbs while he and his friends were all bulk. Cass had her aunt's red hair, the same sparks in her look, but her gaze was still quizzical.

"Aunt Marika says I have no history," Cass said. "I can't help it if I was born after the war. 'You cannot possibly understand, you know nothing,' she tells me triumphantly every morning. And then she starts one of her horrible stories—of fear and hiding and misplaced trust and chopping the tails off rats before grilling the bodies for food during the war. Why do *you* say they're terrible, dinner parties? I thought I was the only one to think that."

Stasek listened to her. The young smell clear, like meadows, he thought. He wondered what it would be like to lick her face. "I guess you could say it's the hidden greed," he said. "Dinner parties are congregations of souls wanting something they don't admit: salvation from dailiness, like checking to see if the mail has come. They should leave their desire for transcendence at the door. With their coats."

"Not me," said Cass. "I don't have such desires. I just try to make it through with no major transgressions. And you?" she asked. "Are you full of hidden greed?"

"Oh, I'm completely greedy," he said, gesturing with both

hands. "But I don't hide it. Besides, I'm not trying to escape my dailiness. Perhaps I want to add more."

"I'd prefer to take my food off to some corner," Cass said. "Instead of this public dance, this evenly-spaced cage of sitting up straight." She looked at him briefly, taking in his graying beard, his green eyes. She tried not to look at him too much; she was too comfortable around him. She reached for the candlestick in front of her, picking off the molten wax and kneading it into jade colored balls. Some had dribbled into the carvings around the heavy wooden base: small peasant figures leading cows in a perpetual circle. She dug at it with her fingernails.

Stasek said, "And then, of course, at table we all have our weapons." He lifted his fork and knife, not in the forceless positions used for eating, but projecting from the heels of his fists. The change was startling. "We refrain from using these on each other," he said. "Because we're so civilized." He put down the cutlery and touched her forearm lightly, smiling. "Aren't we?" he said.

"Of course, I am not doing this properly," Zosha lectured. "In the true method, nothing is cooked, and nothing is mixed, even on the plate. Also wine is forbidden. But Jacob would not agree to *that*." She gestured at her husband who was making his way counterclockwise around the table, pouring a white Sancerre.

Tournivelle, beside Zosha, turned to her after finishing his melon. "*Délicieux*," he proclaimed, a slight tremor in his voice. "It reminds me…" he glanced at his reptilian friend, Marion, across the table to see if she could hear him, and started a story about melons, astronomical observatories, Hawaii. Cass tried to listen; these people were always telling stories.

Cass sniffed at the piece of raw pig fat on her fork. It smelt like what was left of bacon if you took away the sweet salty smokiness. Zosha was holding her portion between thumb and index finger of both hands; she sniffed and nibbled, saying, "Ah. Now this is what I consider eating."

Cass didn't want to eat raw fat. She prodded at the greasy smoothness with her fingers. How hard it was to behave when the rules kept being changed. Stasek's knee suddenly pressed against her leg. Some organ of hers gave a leap. She poked more holes in the white strip of fat with her fork. Stasek's knee tapped hers. He said, quietly, "Watch." While everyone else looked at Marika, who was holding forth on a new Polish artist, Stasek covered his pig fat with his hands and lowered them slowly to his lap.

"Where?" Cass said.

"Pocket," he said, softly.

"It's going to be all slimy."

"Half paper napkin."

"How do I do it?"

"Same way. Just wait for the proper moment. It's easier if you rip the napkin first."

Cass filched her own pork fat, tucked it into the waiting napkin on her lap. "It won't go in," she mouthed to Stasek. "My jeans are too tight."

"I have always thought," Stasek said aloud to the rest of

the table. "That women were doing themselves a disservice by wearing jeans that are too tight." There were times when he couldn't avoid simple mischief. "They have to lie down, on the floor, to zip them up."

"Isn't that right, Tournivelle? That jeans should be zipped up while lying on the floor?" Zosha said.

"Eh, Tournivelle? Wake up," said Marion. "We need your opinion as a Frenchman. You're the only one here."

Tournivelle sat up and announced with pride that he had never worn jeans. "Probably Mademoiselle Cass," he said, pointing at her with a finger which wobbled, "is the only one young enough to wear the item in question."

Zosha's husband, Jacob, turned to Cass with a slight smile. "And you my dear, do you also lie down on the floor to get dressed?"

Cass had bought her jeans in Paris, at Marika's urging. A Parisian salesgirl had lectured her on the proper size and dressing habits, the prone position. Cass had replied that she didn't intend to make love to her jeans, simply to get them on. The salesgirl had shrugged.

Closing one eye, Stasek watched Marika at the other end of the table and wondered if she knew that he was courting her niece. He often kept one eye shut. Marika said this was 'To keep the depths out.' But it wasn't that, it was to simplify things by stripping away the third dimension, translating the world into the length and breadth of his photographs. They were both always translating, here in Paris. Polish was the universal language, Marika claimed, although she had been in France all her adult life, since the early years of the war. Yiddish was a subterranean stream. She understood, but never spoke it. It was like a scar that showed only when the light fell a certain way. English she didn't like, but spoke often, to show that she could. What Marika wanted out of life—now, she said, out of middle-aged life in Paris—was a certain craft, a certain craftiness. Knowing where to buy fine leather shoes for almost nothing: this was important to her. She could tell when shipments of toothbrushes made of boar bristle had come to the flea market. Then she would stock up, buying for Stasek, for other friends, for all the visitors she would ever have. She hoarded. In her apartment, drawers were stuffed with bottle corks, ceramic jugs bristled with wooden spoons, carved and plain. When she saw them in the Saturday markets, the spoons called out to her and she claimed she couldn't leave them behind.

Stasek felt that he would always be with Marika.

"Ah. The names of pigments," Marika was saying. "So thick with meaning—you can chew them, almost."

The rest of them were chewing their curly lettuce. Cass tried to listen to her aunt's discourse. Her hand, on the table a palm's width away from Stasek's, seemed to be responding to his, independent of her will. The two hands were dancing beside each other, maintaining closeness, never straying too far lest some pull get too attenuated, some force falling off with the square of the distance. Cass raised her hand to her face, brushing her red hair from her forehead. Her hand took itself back to the table, a little closer to Stasek's. He, not looking, or not seeming to, moved his hand away in parallel. Finally, to end the nonsense, she lifted her hand and put it under her thigh, sitting on it to anchor it.

Now there was the problem of what to do with the pig fat; feeling around the under-surface of the table she found that it would just fit on a strut bracing the corner.

Outside, the lingering sun had turned the stone of the cathedral a warm orange. Along the towers, animals and spirits stood captured in stone, mortared rigid in their architectural dance, held back from moving, held back from falling.

"I keep telling my niece that leather should be worn on the feet," Marika said. "Not rubber. Not nylon. Those only un-shape the foot."

"Ah yes," said Zosha. "Bent feet: bent mind. Not bent, perhaps... how do you say?"

"Warped?" said Marion.

"Yes. She will warp," Zosha said. "Why do you not take her to buy some proper shoes, Marika?"

Cass began to itch. Her toes flexed in her sneakers. She wanted to go outside. She wanted to smash a brick of cook-ing chocolate with a hammer, and eat the pieces; then she would need black coffee, strong and skunklike. Her body seemed to be leaning toward Stasek. She pulled herself up: chair close to the table, voice low and soft, drinking when they drank, eating when they ate. This was a concert of intake, a forced seated minuet. Everyone was so old here.

Stasek said, "Relax. Be still."

"I am still," she said. "Don't you ever feel," she asked him, "that you do what you're told too often? Why is Zosha eating like this, anyway? Listen, do you think you could take me out for dinner sometime?"

Stasek put his hand lightly on Cass's wrist. "Do you ever feel..." he paused. "That you should ask just one thing at a time?"

"It's swarming in there," she said, pointing to her forehead, grinning. "You're lucky I'm so restrained."

Stasek paused, thinking that what he wanted at that moment was to be in a small confined space with Cass—an old Parisian elevator, wrought iron and varnished wood, going slowly up seven floors. He said, "This diet is Zosha's way of paying back Marika for *her* sortie into vegetarianism last year. Instead of wine, Marika served thermos bottles of artichoke water at each meal." He made a face. "It was foul."

"Are they in competition, then, Marika and Zosha? Why do they do this? I suppose you're going to say I wouldn't understand." Her voice was shaky. She didn't know why she was so wound up. "I suppose you're going to say it's got something to do with eating rats." She tried to keep her voice low. "Marika is always telling me about her brilliant menu of vermin during the war, and she wasn't even in Poland; she was just in France. Nothing makes me want to work on my Physics as much as Marika starting in on her life. She says I don't listen. What does she want from me? What is she trying to do by telling me? It's as though we're in some kind of competition for who has had the most horrible life. Or even the longest one. But I haven't had a horrible life, so what am I supposed to do? I wonder if people on this diet eat cadavers. Do you think so? I suppose Zosha ate rats, too. Does that explain it? Did you eat rats?"

Stasek clamped his hand over hers, holding it tightly to the table. "Stop it," he said. "You don't know anything."

Cass could not stop. "Ah. So you say that, too," she said. "Am I going to have to listen to your stories? Am I going to have to look under your bandages, too?" She pulled her hand from under his. Not daring to look at him, she got up, excused herself and left the table.

Marion looked startled as Cass came into the kitchen. She was stirring bits of pork, peppers, onions, tomatoes, in a skillet on the stove. "The bathroom is there." She pointed toward the corridor with her wooden spoon.

Cass nodded. In the bathroom she filled the sink with cold water, and held back her hair while she dipped her face, keeping it in the water as long as she could. She lifted her head, shook it, dried her face on a purple towel which smelled of Zosha's smoky perfume. Then she took off her jeans and urinated in the bidet, drying herself on the same towel.

Going back into the dining room Cass realized that the only part of dinner parties she ever liked was when she absented herself from the table. As she sat down, she felt Stasek's knee against hers.

"Are you all right?" he asked.

"Much better. Look, I'm sorry about all that. I can be pretty awful."

"We all can. Don't worry. We can talk about it later—if you want. There will be time. Old lady in there, cooking up a tempest?"

"We say, 'cooking up a storm.'"

Eight bright tomatoes on a white oval platter.

"When things are too finely chopped," Zosha was saying, "they change state. Oxidation flows in. Carrots, for example, should never be grated. All those tiny, orange carrot surfaces for oxygen to react on." She fluttered her fingers. "Smell these tomatoes, please," she said. "It is better not to cut them."

Cass felt nostalgic for grilled meat. Obediently, she held her tomato to her nose and turned toward Stasek to see if he was doing the same.

Stasek was looking at Cass, at her arms. He wanted to run his cheek over them, to lick them. He wanted to run his finger around the neck of her mustard yellow t-shirt. He wanted to touch the back of her neck. He turned away from her and remarked to Zosha about the redness of the smell of the tomato.

As Stasek talked to Zosha, Cass let her knee drift against his. When he didn't move away, she, too, wanted to exclaim about something. She kept quiet, biting into the redness of the tomato.

Zosha passed the cobalt blue plate of avocados. Jacob began to reminisce about old-style French cooking, marriages of animals and alcohol, he called it. How well certain foods went with wine. He murmured that even the stark-naked avocado in front of him would copulate with a hay-scented Chardonnay. Cass thought she could feel Jacob's thigh edging toward her.

"Ah, rabbit," Marika exclaimed. "Rabbit in chartreuse. Did I ever tell you about our cooking during the war?"

Stasek saw that Cass was about to answer; he touched her arm. "Be still," he said. "Let her do it." Cass looked down at her half-eaten avocado, wishing for oil and vinegar, wishing to be absent.

"It wasn't just rats," Marika began. "We had all the vermin, many other. We would stew them in chartreuse when there still was any, or other liqueurs, and finally in wine, olive oil until it ran out, and always herbs. All the old French recipes can be adapted to rodents. Naturally, we had also special combinations: rosemary for otters, for example, it takes away the fishy oils; lemon verbena for water rat. Rabbit, ah! King of the rodents. There were never any rabbits."

Cass turned to Stasek. "Why is she telling this? Haven't they all heard it?"

Before Stasek could answer, Jacob interrupted. Cass winced; she wanted to be able to talk to Stasek but here were all these others, swooping in like bats, carving up the evening sky.

"Twenty-two." Jacob persisted. "Tell me, what does it feel like to be twenty-two?"

Cass did not know the correct answer. "Well," she said.

"Like mustard. It feels like mustard on bread, in a cafe. How does it feel to be your age?" she asked. "Whatever that is."

"Half past fifty," he said. "It feels decadent and sublime."

Cass thought that in him it looked more like rotting wood, like an old wharf at the edge of the river.

"But enough of decadence," Jacob said. "At last, now, I get to look at the American Niece."

Cass shifted in her chair. She wished everyone didn't have titles for her. He was breathing on her. His teeth were narrow and brown. Two weeks earlier he had asked her on the phone if she would come to the window of her aunt's apartment so that he could look at her. She had refused; she had felt invaded by the request. Now his thigh rested against hers. He was much too close.

"So much black, the students are wearing, so many layers of cotton," Zosha was saying.

"They seem to love filth," Marika said. "It's no good unless it's torn and dirty. Clothes are not ready for the laundry if they still have clean spots."

Cass knew these remarks were directed at her. She was bewildered that they could find so much fault with her.

"My sister," Marika was saying. "My sister buys a dress for Cass each year, as a birthday present. Ever since the girl was twelve years old and became a woman. But will she wear them?" Marika pointed at Cass. "Ah no. They gather in her closets, lined up like years."

Cass blushed. She wondered why it gave her aunt so much pleasure to denounce her.

Stasek placed his hand on Cass's thigh. At first it was simply to steady her, as one would a nervous animal, half wild.

Cass smiled. She wondered if Stasek was really serious about her aunt, and if he was, how he could be. She liked his hand on her; it seemed to indicate a way out, it would lead her through the maze of behavior.

Finally the women stopped discussing clothes and shifted into Polish. Jacob said to Cass, "Well, Twenty-Two, did you leave a boyfriend behind in the States? Do you have one here in Paris?"

Older people always wanted to know. He would wait for her to blush. He would try to find out if she was a virgin, though he would not ask directly. He would say she didn't understand what he was asking. She would make a lewd gesture to show that she knew what he had in mind. He would pretend to be hurt by her crudeness. Then, with a mixture of reverence and cynicism, he would try to prove that she didn't really know anything about love: fleeting, and passion: consuming.

Cass had a sort of boyfriend, from the physics seminar, but he was too serious about her while she regarded him with tolerant amusement; it was not love, not passion, but a cushion, really, against solitude. She didn't want to discuss this with Jacob. It would be abetting middle-aged prurience. "Why don't we talk about you instead," she said. "Why don't we talk about *your* pillow life."

When Jacob's hand found its way to her other thigh, Cass tried not to jump.

Marion, back from the kitchen, rubbed her hands and began speaking to Cass about caves in the south of France. The old woman's voice dropped as she got more excited, and Cass had to lean forward to hear her. While they talked, Cass kept her own hands on the table as she ever so slowly brought her thighs together, waiting for the moment when Stasek's and Jacob's hands would touch.

With a loud cough, Jacob pulled back his chair. "Will you excuse me?" he said. He muttered something about the toilet and left the table.

"What happened?" Cass asked Stasek, below the general buzz.

"I pinched his hand, slapped it away. Disgusting old lecher."

"And you?"

"Younger, and much less disgusting."

"But you're my aunt's lover."

"Ah. So. Another point in my favor."

Outside, in the last of the evening light, a flock of pigeons wheeled, turning white and then dark again, casting a momentary glimmer into the room.

Stasek got up to help Zosha clear the plates for the next course. "You sit, Zosha. We'll take care of it," he said, nodding to include Cass.

In the kitchen Cass found some little bottles of spices. They seemed clandestine. She shook nutmeg and cayenne and rosemary into her palm, rubbed them together with her index finger, licked it. Stasek, who had been carrying in plates and stacking them by the sink, came up behind her.

"What are you making?" he said.

She held out her palm to him. He licked it. "Let's see the other," he said. She held it out to him.

"But this one is empty," he said. He licked her palm. He kissed it. She drew back.

"Come here," he said.

"Where?"

"Here." He pulled her beside him at the sink, standing so that their bodies touched from shoulder to ankle as he began to wash the plates.

"But you're my aunt's lover," she repeated.

"Among others."

Cass pulled away. "Shit," she said. "Is that supposed to make it better or worse?"

"For you? Less guilt toward your aunt," he said. "But more jealousy." Then he added, "If you have tendencies towards jealousy."

"I don't know," she said. "But then, as you all keep telling me, I don't know anything." She paced to the other side of the room. "Look," she said. "I'm really sorry for bursting out like that about the rats. You all seem to understand each other. I do try to listen to Marika, but sometimes I wonder if her stories can cause new craziness as well as document what has already happened. And then I try to think about all that pain, and it turns into a question of damage of nerves—cells of the body, cells of the brain—and I find myself floating further and further into abstraction, away from the concrete human hurt that she is trying to expose me to, and it no longer has any connection with anything real." She came back to the sink and looked into the soapy water. "Sometimes," she said. "Sometimes I feel like a different species."

"Yes," he said. He came up behind her and put his hands on her shoulders. Turning her around, he hugged her, and waited until she relaxed into his embrace. "You are a different species. Tonight, as you've probably noticed, you are the scapegoat. You can take it, it won't last. They need you; you're young and radiant and not bent. Besides, goats have many virtues."

"Goats," she said. "Goats get to eat tin cans. We're just eating this raw nonsense. Why are all of you so strange?"

"Who?"

"You old people, living here. I mean, you're not old, but them…" her voice trailed off. She hadn't meant to call him old, he wouldn't like that, although he was probably twice her age.

"No, no," he said. "You can include me with them. We have all been damaged, we have grown like trees desperately curving around a wall of rock. Skirmishes with life which make us complex even as they color us, or contaminate us, I'm not sure which. Don't stay around me too long. I'm as tainted as they are. I use you as a scapegoat as well. What you take as repellent, is, to them—to us—a badge of honor. And the fact that it repels you proves to us, and we need constant proving, that what we have been through, what we are going through, is horrible and glorious and different from what you are."

Although it puzzled her, Cass was attracted by Stasek's explanation. She moved toward him and kissed him lightly on the cheek.

"Oh, god," he said. "Keep your distance. We cannibalize youth."

Cass turned to the sink and gripped its edge. There was no way of straightening the lives of these people. They were formed and misshapen by their stories. She couldn't undo anything for them. She could hardly listen to them and rarely understood. All she could do was try to imagine. She wasn't sure if their horrors were all in the past or were continuing still. All she could do was try to deal with them somehow, to bear them, now—in all their twistedness. She turned back toward Stasek. He put his knuckles so softly against her lips that there was nothing to do but kiss them.

Feeling Cass's lips on his hand, Stasek thought about Marika's need for him. He would stay with Marika, he knew, but for a while, he needed both women. He needed the sweet furious linearity of the younger one to be able to deal with the distorted angles of the other. Of course he was rationalizing his greed. That was what one did with greed. The gravest sin was to hold back from fear of it. Life was too short for such caution. Cass would not stay with him long. Meanwhile he could show her how to listen.

"We will talk about all of this," he said. "There will be time." Then he pointed to the dishes and they began to dry them.

They carried the clean plates back to the dining room. Now Zosha passed a bowl of broad beans, green ribbons an inch wide. Cass slit them apart with her nails and popped out the lima bean sized embryos. They tasted like horse chestnuts and grass. Jacob was safely talking to Marika and Zosha.

"You said 'Among others,'" Cass said to Stasek. "How many others?"

"Aha. We've gotten curious."

"How many?"

"One at a time."

"You know what I mean."

"It's hard to answer. Some are sporadic; some are even rarer than that."

"Does Marika know?"

Zosha interrupted. "Cass dear," she said. "Be an angel, go and find the platters of fish in the refrigerator."

Cass went into the kitchen. If Stasek were here with her she would lead him into the broom closet. They would latch the door behind them and throw themselves into each other's desire among the strange smells: the soap and mildew of sponge mops, the dust and summer grassfields of the cornstalk broom, the furniture polish rags with their healing reek of beeswax and turpentine. They would prop the vacuum cleaner back against the wall when it fell over onto them. She would throw her arms around his neck ready to ride him. "Not here," he would say, kissing her.

"Patience," he would say. He would say, "Wait."

The fish course was thin slices of salmon. The talk was in Polish. It sounded as though they were talking about Japanese cooking, about sashimi.

Zosha passed a cut glass bowl of strawberries. Marika asked her, "I don't suppose you would eat whipped cream with these?"

"Whipped cream?" said Zosha. "I'm afraid not. The whipping is not good. You see, it mixes oxygen into the cream—then you have a mixture, not something that is pure. Oxidation happens so rapidly in that case. And, of course there's another trouble with cream; it is the same as the problem with milk. You see, the cow is a large animal." Zosha pushed back her chair to give herself room to gesture the outline of a huge, airy cow. "Because it is so large, cow's milk is made of very large molecules. We also would become very large if we drank milk from cows."

Cass looked into Zosha's eyes. "What about milk from a smaller animal?" she asked. "What about milk from a goat?"

Zosha looked back at her. "A goat?" she said. "I see, a goat. I don't know. I'll have to find out."

Cass cleared the table. When Stasek appeared in the kitchen, she motioned toward the broom closet. He shook his head. Instead, he opened the door leading from the kitchen to the landing. Stopping for a moment to adjust the latch so that they would not be locked out, he took her hand and led her along the corridor. When they got to the door of the roof garden, he opened it silently and slid it shut behind them.

Outside, night had fallen. Floodlights hit the lacy parapets of the cathedral, outlining the gargoyles. Angels and demons stood out sharply from the minor spires. Cass looked where Stasek was pointing, above the church into the night air, glowing with invisible particles. She finally saw the inverted shadow of the edifice, dark and deep, hovering upside down above it, where the building itself had shielded part of the sky from the lights along its base.

As they shed their clothing, Stasek thought of how he and Cass must appear to the stones of the old cathedral. Perched on railings and waterspouts, the monkeys, goats and griffons would see two figures on the roof detach from the blackness, revealing themselves white and glimmering like sea creatures covered with phosphorescence.

Cass, freed from her clothes, took Stasek's hand and led him across the terrace. "Hold me," she said. "I want to walk up there." She pointed to the cement railing supported by urn-shaped columns which ran around the edge of the roof.

"Are you sure?" he said.

Stasek gripped her wrist hard as she stepped onto a tub of geraniums and from there onto the balustrade. He watched her as she walked on tiptoe along the railing at the edge. Her body glowed pale and full and luminous against the darkness of the sky and the ornate cathedral with its gaunt crouching demons.

Cass paced slowly with both arms outstretched, one still in Stasek's grasp, one over the drop to the ground seven storeys below. Her toes felt the sandy surface of the concrete and occasional patches of tarry substance. The night breeze, thick and warm, played over her skin, ruffled her hair. Stopping for a moment, she looked down at the sidewalks and smiled. Briefly, she wondered if anyone was watching.

When she got to the corner of the balustrade, she turned to face Stasek. "Get me down from here," she said.

He took her in his arms. Hand in hand they stumbled among the potted geraniums to the pile of cushions under the striped awning. She pulled him down on top of her, kissing him fiercely. "I don't like dinner parties," she said, wrapping her arms around his neck and her legs around his legs.

"Dinner parties are terrible," he said as he kissed her face, her neck, her breasts.

From the streets far below a car horn sounded; another answered; a woman's laughing voice called out.

Foreign Things

OUR FAMILY HAS ALWAYS BEEN FULL OF DISTANCES. My brother Thomas left for college when I was eight. When he was through with school he came home to Boston only long enough to pack his things and move to Paris. My father's family is in the south of France and we never see them any more. My mother's sister, Marika, lives in Paris. Their other siblings have scattered themselves across the United States as though choosing to be as separate from each other as possible. Both of my parents still work in museums, separate ones, of course. He is in charge of a classical collection; she takes care of paintings. They no longer take care of each other.

Five years ago, I went to Paris on a fellowship to study Physics. I also felt like a self-appointed emissary to my Aunt Marika, whom I had known as a child but hadn't seen since I was ten. Like the city itself, I found Marika attractive and repelling in equal parts. More important to me than Marika or Paris, though, was the idea of my brother Thomas. I had just turned twenty-two and I had not seen him for a decade.

Now, I wanted to show him my womanhood and my Physics, and I hoped he would want to see everything, just as I wanted to find out who he had become.

I arrived in the city in May and stayed with Marika in her apartment on the Left Bank. In mid-June, I moved out. I had started sleeping with her lover, Stasek, and it was time for me to find a place of my own.

At times I feel stifled by too much good behavior. I've always had trouble in libraries and in the museums where my parents worked. Sometimes during those first weeks in Paris, I would get overpowered by the orderliness of the city: the rows of grey limestone apartments, dark slate roofs, curlicued iron balconies, all those precise repetitions would make me feel disorderly and out of step. Not that I wanted to be anywhere else but Paris, I simply needed to breathe a chaotic air from time to time. Then Thomas would tell me to go to the raucous Avenue de Belleville to eat a couscous with the Tunisian Jews, or to bathe with large Arab ladies in the *Hammam* of the Paris Mosque—and I would do what he said and feel much better afterwards, always wondering how he knew all these obscure crannies, how long it had taken him to reach that point, and whether I could ever approach it.

The day that I moved out of Aunt Marika's, I telephoned Thomas at the small wine store he owned on the Left Bank.

His shop was quite successful, partly, I guess, because of the oddity of an American daring to run a wine shop in France. As I told him about my new place, he sounded glad to hear my voice and he reminded me that I was invited to dinner that night to celebrate his birthday; he was thirty-two.

I spent the rest of the afternoon after the solid-state seminar shopping for a present for Thomas. I couldn't bring wine, I didn't dare buy clothes: he wore Italian pants and leather jackets soft as butterscotch caramels. He smoked only occasionally: thin cigars, imported from the east.

When it started to rain, I ducked into the Vietnamese grocery in my neighborhood. I wanted to chat with the owner, Madame Hanh, and to inhale the salty, dirty fragrance of dried fish; the sheaves of fresh lemon grass that smell citrussharp when you slit the stalks with your thumbnail; and coriander, green and slightly acrid, reminding me a bit of armpits.

Madame Hanh had a broad smile revealing a gold tooth right in front. Her hair hung in a gray braid almost to her waist. Across the street was the Vietnamese restaurant run by her family. Sometimes in the late afternoons she would take me there to visit, leaving one of her daughters-in-law in charge of the grocery.

In the back of the dimly lit restaurant all the older women sat at a round table, rolling the tightly packed Vietnamese 'rouleaux de printemps,' those raw spring rolls stuffed with shrimp and mint and beansprouts. They would ask me in strongly accented French about my family, my studies, my friends. I told them about Jean-Claude, a physics student I was seeing occasionally, but I let them know that was not serious. I didn't tell them anything about Stasek. Their family structure is so different, they wouldn't have liked my hanging out with my aunt's lover who was twenty years older than I was. They wouldn't have understood how I started to fall in love with him the afternoon that Marika was painting my nude portrait and she had invited him to come and watch, using my nakedness for her own courtship purposes. As soon as I realized what she was doing, I didn't think I had to hold back with Stasek. That year I took what I wanted. I also gave, whatever I wanted. You could do that, then.

There, in the Vietnamese restaurant, the women would talk to me of their children and chide me about my lack of plans for marriage. When I left them I could hear their talk shift back into the singsong cadence of Vietnamese.

I told Madame Hanh I needed a birthday present for my brother. She swept her arms wide in a gesture inviting me to take the whole grocery. White canvas sacks of rice, small jars of chili paste, bottles of fermented fish sauce—nothing seemed appropriate. Finally, over in a corner, I saw a stack of large green fruits covered with pyramidal spikes. They were the size of large coconuts but looked more reptilian than vegetal, like the egg a dinosaur might lay. Trying to pick one up, I found it so heavy that the spines bit into my palms. I pulled down the sleeves of my jacket to cover my hands and lifted it.

Madame Hanh at the register saw what I was doing and whooped with laughter. "No, Mademoiselle Cass. Foreigners don't like this fruit. The French, the Americans, never."

"What is it?" I asked.

"*De rien,*" was what I thought she said. Nothing at all.

"*Arrivé ce matin. De Malaysie,*" she explained. Just in this morning, from Malaysia.

"Yes, but what is it called?" I tried again.

"*De rien,*" she repeated.

I asked her the price and she shook her head as she told me, "*Cent francs.*"

A hundred francs was twenty dollars, then. Of course it was outrageous for a single piece of fruit, but it seemed correctly outlandish for Thomas. I hoped he would see the geometric beauty in the array of its green thorns.

I paid for my "Nothing-at-all" and asked Madame Hanh how to eat it. Wrapping it in newspaper and coaxing it into a paper bag, she told me what to do with the seeds as well as the flesh.

I didn't want to arrive at Thomas's place too early—he's rather precise about time—so I went into the café of the Paris Mosque which is just around the corner. The fig trees behind the metal-studded wooden gate were in full leaf. The rain had stopped; the air already had the softness of early summer as the sun angled over the rim of the white stucco walls and filled the courtyard with yellow light.

I ordered an Arabic coffee, placing the reptilian fruit, its spines poking through the bag, on the chair beside me. Then I settled back to examine the other café-sitters.

Gait and posture interest me. I try to figure out what pain is being avoided by that slight hesitation of the left foot, what new love causes the irrepressible play of that flickering smile. Nationalities show up in the way people sit. I could tell the French by their rectilinear attitudes: the way they gestured only with their hands and forearms, keeping their upper arms tucked close to their bodies as though holding something precious to their sides. The few Americans were loosely tipping back, legs splayed on the diagonal, arms akimbo. There weren't many Arabs this afternoon, only the waiter shuffling out from the kitchen in his soft felt slippers.

Thomas opened the door and hugged me, then kissed me on both cheeks.

"Let's look at you Cass, see if you've changed any."

He always said that. It kept me off balance, a little; I wasn't sure what changes he wanted, except perhaps my clothing. He parted my aviator jacket and took hold of the orange cotton of my t-shirt, rubbing it between thumb and forefinger as if it were fine silk.

"Exquisite, my dear. Where do you find your things?" He knew of course; he had directed me to the flea markets on the northern outskirts of the city. He held the sleeve of my jacket, saying: "Clignancourt—third stall on the left after the African carvings?"

I loved clothes from the flea market, pieces with scars and history, though sometimes when I saw Thomas in all his dark-eyed beauty, wearing his cufflink shirts and linen trousers, I would wonder if there was some reason—aside from the smallness of my fellowship stipend—why I was always such a mess.

Thomas's Italian friend, Bernardo, gave me greeting kisses.

He worked in the ethnology museum, on Etruscan sculpture. He put an arm around me, playfully, and I wanted him to leave it there. I was always attracted to my brother's friends.

"You don't look half bad, Cass, child. How's school? Still hunting for mistakes in crystals?"

"Not mistakes, Bernardo. Dislocations: different arrangements. Regular arrangements don't teach you anything..."

I would have gone on, but Elena, Thomas's current woman, appeared beside us.

"Ah. There you are," she said. She had been arranging a vase of red snapdragons. She held me by the shoulders, examining me as though I were a new life form which lacked some necessary attribute, and finally brushed my cheeks with kisses.

"You look fine, Cass; really you do." Elena was usually morbidly quiet whenever I came over. It might have been shyness, but I always thought it was because, in her Yugoslav way, she perceived sad ironies that none of the rest of the world suspected. Occasionally when I saw her sitting alone in a café I would join her for a bit, but I usually felt she was trying to tell me about something that I wasn't ready to hear yet. She and Thomas had been together, on and off, for about a year; I didn't know whether they were on, now, or off. I was always afraid she was dragging him down.

The doorbell sounded. It was Thomas's friend, Marion, an ancient anthropologist who held some high position in Bernardo's museum. We really couldn't get away from museum people, Thomas and I. Marion had something to do with prehistoric caves in southern France. She had been a friend of my father's parents, and though originally American, she was crusted over with Frenchness. Standing critically straight, elbows tight to her waist, she put both her creased hands around mine in greeting. Then she opened her black handbag and took out a box of chocolates the size of a gold ingot; this made me remember my own offering.

I found my sac where I had left it by the door and unwrapped the fruit from its damp bag, cleaning torn bits of newspaper from between the spikes. "This is for your birthday," I said to Thomas. "I hope it's okay."

"Oh," said Elena. "Is one really to eat such a thing?"

Thomas gave a pleased grin. "Well, Cass," he said. "This is a rare treat."

"Madame Hanh at the Vietnamese grocery says it's called *De Rien*. She said that, actually, animals like them, too, and sometimes the men harvesting them from the trees will be scooped up, in turn, by an elephant."

Thomas corrected me gently. "Actually it's called *durian*. Not everybody can stand it, but I'll let you have some when it's ripe." I would have been crushed that he knew of it already, but he seemed so pleased, and gave such a mischievous smile, and finally put his hand on my shoulder saying, "Now you deserve a glass of wine."

Bernardo was in the kitchen alcove washing little clams. When Thomas gave one of his dinners, Bernardo liked to manage the cooking, usually pasta with small marine animals mixed in. Bernardo's wife had gone back to Italy for a visit of indeterminate length; he didn't like to talk about her.

"Cass, child," Bernardo said. "Bring your wine and come and tell me everything and I'll let you chop the garlic."

I liked Bernardo and would have told him anything. I

started with a lecture I had just attended—about defects in
the crystalline structure which act as conduits to the center
of the crystal from the outside. Bernardo finally touched my
arm and said in a low voice:

"You can speak more softly, little one. Your brother will
hear you if he wants to."

I looked down at the pile of garlic I was cutting. Blushing, I continued, almost in a whisper, until we got to the edge
of what you can explain without diagrams.

"What's going on in the rest of your life?" Bernardo asked.
"Still seeing your aging Polish fellow?"

"He's only forty or so."

"For you—that's moribund. What does Auntie Marika
think about this?"

"Nothing, I hope. I'm not about to tell her, and Stasek's
rather afraid of her."

"You seeing anyone else? That student?"

I nodded.

"Good. He is more suitable. More your age."

"I don't know. He feels young to me. He doesn't know
anything. I need somebody more…"

"And your new place is too small… but you can't move
in with him because he still lives with his parents, the way
French students do until they either all go mad or go to
America to finish their degrees?"

"Are you asking or telling?"

"Just making sure." He smiled at me. I think I was a bit in
love with Bernardo, too, at that moment.

"Every time he comes over he brings a rose. I hate roses.
I put them in beer bottles and I forget to throw them out.

He's so young, so ardent. I feel inundated. I need an umbrella."

"Perhaps just a new young man."

At dinner, Marion turned to me, saying: "Thomas often talks of you; he says you're quite a bit more intelligent than he is. What a pity you're in physics."

"A pity?"

"For the rest of us. We need new brains in anthropology."

I wasn't sure how to take this. Marion frightened me a little: she had that chameleon quality of people who are at home in places they were not born in. Thomas was getting it, too. It wasn't just a question of language, of tossing it about and being playful with it; they were both deeply comfortable in this city in a way that I was not, even though I had spent time with my grandparents in the south of France as a child. My French was not quite adult yet. I wondered if I would always be an outsider.

I got up and cleared away the pasta plates with their litter of clamshells and dark blue periwinkles. Elena did not cook; she seemed too listless to clean up. I'm not sure she did much of anything that was useful. Bernardo brought in a platter of baked salmon, surrounded by papaya slices. The salad had walnuts and fresh red currants, little explosions of fragrant sourness. What I liked about Thomas was that he didn't make a fuss about the wine; he didn't talk about it, it just appeared and changed at the proper times and provided a certain radiance. I was learning to not let it outpace me.

Bernardo had made the cake at his place: it was dense with ground almonds and bitter chocolate. You had to eat it slowly, with concentration.

"Listen, Cass," Thomas said. "I'm going to Avignon for ten days. Elena is off to Yugoslavia. I was wondering if you wanted to use this place while I'm gone. Or if you could just look in every so often and water the plants."

This was the first time he had trusted me to be there when he was gone. I had always wanted to: you can learn a lot about someone by being in his place alone—rooms send you such different messages when their owners are absent. Also, my apartment was very small. The shower was primitive and leaked down onto my neighbors if I used more than a dribble of hot water. I told Thomas I was honored.

I took away the dessert plates while Bernardo made espresso. As we drank it, Thomas offered around his handrolled Burmese cigars, the ones with filters made of palm leaves.

I returned to Thomas's the next day; I told myself it was to water the plants and to take a shower, but I really wanted to look around.

Thomas's bed was vast, covered with a handwoven spread of blue cotton; nothing under the bed, not even dust animals. On his bookshelves: wine encyclopedias, an atlas of France, rows of paperbacks in French and English, and two photograph albums which I remembered seeing at home when I was a kid. I left those for later, wondering what his view of our family was. I never got around to looking at them. I found myself sponging the black marble counters in the kitchen, sweeping, dusting—though none of these domestic intimacies were really needed. With a rag and some salad oil—walnut, I think—I polished the antique mahogany desk. I was rubbing the place down, caressing it as though it were some large animal.

The following day I was back again, really to water the plants. I took care of the sprawling philodendron and the geraniums. Some flower I didn't recognize had bloomed, suddenly, and its white stars filled the place with their heady sweetness. After I arranged the yellow batik pillows on the couch I poked around inside the desk. I found a picture of myself at college that my mother must have sent him, and a few others of me that I didn't remember ever having seen. I was pleased to find myself inside his desk, mixed in with his letters.

I felt lonely there, and gave Bernardo a call, asking him if he wanted to have a drink with me. I had never telephoned him before. We could drink some of Thomas's wine, I said. If he wanted, he could bring over some food from the catering shop nearby. He said he would prefer to take me out somewhere.

After dinner Bernardo walked me back to Thomas's apartment. "Don't you want to come up?" I asked.

"Cass, child…" he hesitated.

"Why do you call me that?"

"It helps keep you in perspective," he said. He put his hands on both my shoulders and held them tightly, keeping me close but not as close as I wanted to be to him. "You need some, too," he said. "You don't know what you're after."

I stayed at Thomas's that night. In the stereo I found a tape of American blues. I turned it up so it began to throb; a woman's voice was singing:

Well, I pull back the covers,
My bed is full of rocks,
Ain't got no more lovers,
This old world is too mean...

On the fourth day I didn't get back to Thomas's place until twilight. When I let myself in, there was a strange smell: a heavy mix of old blue cheese and grapes, moldy onions and swamp gas.

The black marble counter-top of the kitchen alcove was clear, but in the corner on the floor was my plastic bag with the fruit in it. You could almost see the fumes pulsing out. I felt dumb; a platter of fresh Vietnamese spring rolls would have been a much better gift for him—all that green mint and beansprouts.

Unlatching the floor-to-ceiling French windows and fanning them back and forth to bring in the evening breeze didn't clear the air, it just seemed to swirl the odors around. Was this what Madame Hanh meant when she said we would be able to smell when it was ready?

I approached it with an open black garbage bag, the way you corner a small wild animal found in the kitchen at night. Once I had it captured, though, I noticed that knotting the bag didn't really help, because the spines pierced both the plastic and the brown paper bag.

Then I heard a key in the lock.

"Oh, Cass," Thomas said. "You're here. I didn't meant to burst in on you without warning. I came back to Paris to meet someone at noon and it took longer than I expected."

I felt like I had been caught out at something. Thomas, too, was acting a bit uncomfortable. "What have you got there?" he grinned. "Not throwing out my durian, are you?"

"But... it smells."

"Let me change my clothes and we'll eat it. See if you can get it out of the bag, and find us a platter."

We sat on the floor in the living room leaning against the couch. Thomas looked sweet and completely scruffy in sweat pants and an old black turtleneck jersey. I had never seen him like that before.

"Ready?" he asked.

I nodded. He took a cleaver and split the fruit along one of its seams. It broke neatly, showing seeds the size of chestnuts. The smell was sweet and awful and fermented—like silage, like sewage, like garlic and maybe corpses—but also full of flowers. I wasn't sure I was going to be able to stay beside him. "Watch," he said, as he pulled out a seed and put it on the platter, then with his three middle fingers scooped out the flesh, and ate it. "Oh, Cass, it's good. It's perfect. Try it." He told me that people say there is a stretch of nine hours when the taste of this kind of durian is at its peak. Before that, it's sour, and after, it's fermented. I felt privileged that we had found the time. I asked him how he knew about it. "An Indonesian lady friend," he said. "She had a motor-cycle... mainly at night, we... she... sometime I'll tell you about it." He paused, noticing that I was holding back. "Do it, Cass," he said.

I put my fingers in. It was a rosy, yolky yellow-orange. I scooped some out. Experiencing that fruit is hard to describe, but I feel if I can pin it down it will be easier for me to describe other things. It felt like a custard, except that we usually don't dabble in custard; more fluid than avocado, softer than papaya, just barely holding its form in my palm, more delicately colored than mango, and smoother. It felt forbidden to be fingering it. It was like the rest of Paris I saw that year—I never got to see the Paris I had heard about in the States. It was as though I had come somewhere else. I never missed that other Paris—the one that other people saw, the normal one. I just hoped I wouldn't be questioned about it, because I wouldn't know what to answer. For me, Paris was sitting on the floor beside Thomas, doing this.

I managed to eat. At first I held my nose to be able to get the scoops of custardy durian close enough to my mouth. The taste was completely different: peaches and almonds and sherry. Finally I found I could simply eat it.

When we had consumed all we could, Thomas said we should think about cleaning up. We would need showers, he said, and we should get rid of the rinds and remains as they would go bad quickly. I wrapped everything in the garbage bag I had been using earlier and offered to take it all down to the bins. The rickety iron elevator in the hallway responded so slowly that I ran down the five flights of stairs.

In the courtyard, I opened the wooden doors one after another to see where the garbage was kept. I was just pulling out one of the orange-capped trash containers when the concierge started yelling from her glass door.

"*Ah, non, non et non.* What do you think you are doing?"

"It's all right, Madame," I called to her. "I'm Monsieur Thomas's sister; I'm just getting rid of something."

She crossed the courtyard, eager to see what I was up to. Then she smelled it.

"*Ah, non.* I knew it. *Non.* You take your obscure garbage out of here. Pick-up is not until tomorrow morning, and that thing will smell up the whole courtyard. *Ah, non.* It is exactly what, anyway?"

She backed off as I unwrapped it to show her. Thomas had never liked her; she yelled at his guests and often refused to sort the mail for days. I approached her, my package open.

"It's a fruit," I said, extending my arms. "Direct from the tropics of the Orient."

"Stick to local products, Mademoiselle. Foreign things often stink."

I re-knotted the bag and carried it across the courtyard and out into the street. The usual accordionist nodded to me as the crowd around him swayed, parting smoothly to let me through. I hurried to avoid two policemen strolling in my direction. The night still had a touch of warmth and the sky had turned purple. The street lights had come on.

I began to worry about my aviator jacket. I was afraid the spines of the fruit were pricking it. I didn't mind the scars, it had plenty already, but I wondered if the spines could inject their smell.

My side of the river was blocked off by moored barges, so I walked upstream towards Notre Dame until I reached an open esplanade paved with cobblestones. Necking couples were evenly spaced along the water's edge. In the pools of light cast by street lamps, some pairs sat almost primly; but further away from the lights the bodies were more entwined, and from the deep shadows by the embankment wall came all the moans and yearnings of an early summer night. Walking on the edge of the quai to a spot with the most space between couples I ached with loneliness and desire, but didn't know who I wanted. I held the garbage bag by its neck and started to swing it back and forth. On the forward swing the remains of the fruit broke through its coverings and flew into the water. The bags went in after it. At first it seemed to sink, but then the green oval sections bobbed slowly to the surface and inserted themselves into the current. All the way back along the esplanade, smells of swamp and turpentine and overripe flowers followed me.

Thomas had bathed and was standing by the open window, smoking. "Do you want to shower?" he asked. "I'll find some clothes for you."

In the shower, I poured dark green Italian shampoo all over me. His razor was gold-colored and smooth on my legs. He had left me a stack of dry towels. After drying myself I found a small blue bottle of after-shave and slathered it on.

Thomas came into the bedroom. I had nothing on, just a towel around my head. I didn't know whether to hide my nakedness or to strut about, so I did neither. I took a deep breath and faced him as though we didn't know each other. "What should I wear?" I asked. He handed me a pair of jockey shorts and I grimaced and put them on.

"Dark or light pants?" he asked, then before I could answer, "I think light would be better. Here." He handed me a pair of his linen trousers; I had to roll the bottoms up. When I bent over, the towel started unwinding from my head and I had an urge to drape it around my neck to hide my breasts, but it was too late for that. I'm not normally very shy, but I felt disoriented being in his place, in his bedroom, getting into his clothes, and having him look at me. He was definitely watching, and I was performing for him and pretending that I wasn't. I gave him the towel, saying, "You take this; it's too damp to put on the bed."

He opened a drawer and handed me a yellow tank top. Then he stood back against the bedroom door, holding my wet towel, watching. I faced him and put it on as though I wasn't doing it for him, trying to avoid both slinkiness and undue grace. When I tucked it into the trousers, he took out an olive green shirt and gave it to me without a word. I didn't say anything; by this time I was gawky and all elbows. My actions were getting slower and slower. The sleeves were much too long.

"Cufflinks," he said. He came over to the dresser and looked in a carved wooden box until he found some cufflinks made of agate and gold. I held out my hands to him, as he rolled my cuffs. As he fastened them I noticed that he, too, was working very slowly. Something had happened to time and it was no longer behaving properly. I felt suddenly panicky and wildly happy and scared.

He took a step back and looked at me. "Hair," he said. I took the hairbrush and tried to regain my former tempo. I did what I normally do, three or four quick strokes.

He made a single *tsk* of disapproval. Taking the brush from me he started working my hair slowly, as though he were angry, or possibly thinking something through.

"Hey?" I said. After that he brushed it more calmly, to dry it. My head began to tingle. He slowed down even more, raising the hair into the air and catching it from underneath. It was more of a caress.

Then he put his hands on my shoulders and turned me toward the mirror: olive shirt and linen pants, brushed reddish-yellow hair, and Thomas, behind me, auburn and dark-eyed and interesting. Compared to him I'm usually kind of ordinary-looking, but I didn't look like myself—I was golden. There was a close resemblance between us that I had never noticed, the planes of the cheekbones and the darkness of the eyes and the way we had both suddenly turned serious, terrified of what was happening to us. He stood watching me in the mirror. His hand was resting on the back of my neck. I looked down at my bare feet. I looked up into the mirror again and saw that he was still watching.

The Lights of Love

NIGHT IN SINGAPORE. A LITTLE MORE THAN ONE DEGREE north of the equator; so hot and damp that if I snap my fingers, the heavens will precipitate. The night is filled with smells: curried turnovers frying in the open-air food stalls; jasmine; sandalwood smoke curling through a hedge as our motorbike passes a hidden shrine. At a stoplight our exhaust catches up with us; a Malay in a white shirt walks by, smoking a clove cigarette. The moon is one night before full.

This may turn out to be important, the moon spreading itself over the city. Though it has taken me a long time to realize, light is now what determines things for me.

"Cass, don't lean into the turns," Max says. He is the husband of one of my oldest friends.

"I'm not," I say. Not wanting to hold him, I grip the metal bar behind my seat. This is the first of our excursions.

"Chinatown," he says. The buildings here are pastel green, lit with dim fluorescent strips. There is something odd about the fluorescence spilling into the night, both inside and out, not contained, and something almost organic about the way everything repeats, the facades with their slightly ornate cornices, the open ground-floor store fronts and the living quarters upstairs, windows open, each looking like the next—the whole row of them reminds me of the segmented bodies of insects, lightning bugs. It is that same sort of cool green glow, mysteriously alive.

We swerve left onto a street lined with trestle tables under dangling low watt bulbs. The tables are piled with spiny green fruit, the size of pumpkins or fresh coconuts. The fruit gives off a sweet and frightening stench, like flowers on the attack, like decay, blue cheese, sherry. "Durian," I say.

"You know it? You've eaten it?"

"In Paris, twenty years ago. Only once. I'll tell you later." That durian I ate with my brother Thomas when I was young and thoughtless, and I believed that my sorrows would forever be the result of my own transgressions. Durian grows here on the Malay Peninsula and all over South East Asia, but in Paris, it was singular, strange, out of place. After sharing it with my brother, I never came into contact with another one, and it is both disconcerting and exhilarating to see, and smell, so many of them at once.

Max parks the bike and we walk along the malodorous street. Chinese and Malay men pick over the green fruits, lifting them to their ears and shaking them to listen. They wear leather gloves to protect them from the spines.

"Only men shop for durian," says Max. "They think it's too important to let women do it."

"Why do they shake them?"

"Listening for air pockets; when you can hear the seeds

shake, they're ripe." At the end of the rows of durian is a single table with a fruit I've never seen, like squat eggplants, but apple-sized, brownish-purple. "Mangosteen," Max said. "I won't tell you what it tastes like, except that it's amazing. You're supposed to follow durian with it, it clears your mouth, your brain."

We buy a small durian and a dozen mangosteen to go with it, putting them in a backpack which Max has lined with folded newspaper. As we ride home, the pack shifts from side to side on my back, whenever we make a turn.

Over dinner of leftover rice—neither of us cares terribly much about cooking—I start to tell Max about the year I spent in Paris when I was in my early twenties. I tell him about the evening in Paris my brother Thomas and I ate durian together and became lovers; to get the smell of the fruit off, we had showered, then things turned larking and serious; finally, flooded with desire for each other and defiance towards everyone else, we decided to make up for our childhood spent apart.

Why do I tell Max so much about my past when I have only just met him? I arrived here in Singapore this morning, in time to see his wife, Megan, for a few hours before she left for Jakarta to attend a conference on tropical fevers. She and I grew up together in Boston. Our travels have kept us apart for years; we write each other long sporadic letters. She wanted me to come now, even though she will only be here for the second week of my visit. It is important to her, she says, that Max and I get to know each other.

Actually, I prefer husbands and wives separately. When I am together with both of them there are too many lines of force, and I feel as though I have to keep everybody in equilibrium by weeding my way through the shifting alliances and forays of group conversation. It's so much simpler to be with one or the other. This does not mean I prefer unmarried men, quite the reverse: married men, particularly those who are happily married, know about love in a way that makes single men seem innocent and unaware and full of striving. It is the same with single women. I think I am the only exception.

So Megan has gone off to lecture about reviving dehydrated infants with a mixture of salts and sugars; the optimal mixture turns out to be very close—the chemists have recently shown—to the composition of chicken soup. Here in Singapore it is school vacation, and their two children are visiting Max's parents in another part of the city. The world has conspired to leave us alone together in this house overlooking a steep hillside jungle.

Max and I have finished our durian. He puts the rinds out in the garden for the mynah birds. With a sharp knife he cuts around each mangosteen and lifts the cap off, revealing the pale translucent segments inside. He shows me how to spoon them out, and the taste is of strawberry, peach, pineapple. I'm glad we bought so many, because I can't get enough of this taste. I lick the inside of the rind: sharply astringent— perhaps that's why it's useful after the custardy richness of durian. Watching my greedy progress through the mangosteen, Max asks, "How long did it last with your brother? How did it end? What were you doing in Paris, anyway?"

What made us quit being lovers, Thomas and me? What makes any of us decide things? Often it's something that seems totally irrelevant at the time, some small absurdity triggers a cascade of decisions, while the rational indicators, which ought to have shown us the way, point like disregarded one-way signs in abandoned neighborhoods.

The impetuous tempo of Max's questions makes me feel a bit frenetic. This is how I explain myself, to Max, that first night. This how I tell him the story of that leaving.

I was in Paris for the year after college. I was supposed to be studying physics, and I was, a bit, but I had also gotten lured into working on a research project in a biophysics lab. I spent all my afternoons on the electron microscope. I was looking at twisted biological forms of liquid crystals, a state of matter halfway between the order of crystals and the disorder of liquids. The room was kept dark because what I had to see was so dim.

The microscope I used was an old German model, made by Siemens. Michel, who was in charge of all the microscopes, showed me how to run it, how to cajole the condenser into alignment until its lopsided blob-like image was centered and round. The controls on those old machines were high on the central column, perverse knobs that made electromagnets shift the electron beam. Perverse, because of age, but also due to the physics of electromagnets—there is a strange lag between cause and effect, as though it takes them a certain time before they decide to act.

Once the condenser was centered, you had to align the other lenses until the beam formed brilliant cusps of light:

you shift "the baby's bottom" cusp into a symmetric trefoil knot, then a three pointed star.

When I worked on the microscope, the only light besides the screen was a red safe-light; the structures I was after— gray shadows on the yellow-green phosphor of the viewing screen—looked like ripples on the bottom of the sea.

I wore sunglasses when I came out of the microscope room, so I wouldn't lose my dark adaptation under the fluorescent lights with their side-eyed flicker and subliminal hum. How did I do it, stay inside at the end of spring when all the air in Paris is green with pollen? I scuttled sideways like a crab, from one darkened room to another, drunk with love of microscopes and crystals, and with love for my brother Thomas.

Each day, on my way to the photographic darkroom where I developed the plates I had taken, I had to pass Michel's room. He was a bearded, bandy-legged man from the south of France whose job it was to keep the machines in working order. Men like this, with a mysterious talent for fixing things, seem to adopt laboratories the way trolls adopt deserted country bridges. Their appointments are never quite regular; you don't find them on the usual payroll. And they can repair even the most archaic equipment.

Michel would sit in his room, smoking, poring over coils and capacitors and other things he had wheedled apart. The room smelled of WD-40, vacuum pump oil, and more obscure lubricants. I wondered whether his genius for knowing how to make things work made up for the perpetual dirt which seemed to cling to him, the smears of graphite on his fingertips, the flecks of ash dropping from yellowed cigarettes whenever he leaned over some delicate part.

Michel seemed to be on the lookout for me each time I passed. He would beckon or grab for me, commenting on my orange or ochre-colored clothes and the redness of my hair, conjecturing about my tendencies in bed. I avoided him when I could.

One day, though, I had to visit, to give him a specimen-holder with a broken hinge. The room was in shadow, a high intensity lamp clamped to his desk illuminated only his bearded face and a metal cylinder covered with parallel fins made of some brassy alloy. Michel looked at the piece I brought and worked it back and forth, then placed it carefully on his work table. Without saying anything, he reached for my hand, turning it over, palm up, the way a fortune teller would. There had never been anything more than banter between us, even when we spent hours together in the darkness of the microscope room, when he was training me. Physically, I was not interested in him. So why did I not pull my hand away from his grasp? I think I saw his action as a kind of dare, he had accused me so often of being afraid of him. I asked him if he thought he could fix the specimen holder.

He ignored my question and continued tracing along my palm with his forefinger. Finally he pushed my hand from him, saying, "You shouldn't let me tease you like this."

There didn't seem to be a good answer, a non-suggestive one. Instead I asked him why I was having so much trouble with focussing the microscope.

"After the first hundred plates," he said, "you'll be fine. But no cheating: you can't just snap pictures." He stopped to light one of his yellowish cigarettes. "You have to throw your heart into each exposure. You have to make love to each field." He watched me as he said this, as though to gauge my reaction.

I gave a kind of noncommittal grunt.

"Here, give me that hand again."

I relinquished my hand to him. He turned it over once more, examining my fingertips. I felt that irrational wonder that comes when someone tells us what our palms imply, as though our hands reveal to others what they persist in hiding from us. "Traces of pigment on your nails. What have you been up to?" He said it as though accusing me of a betrayal.

"I was visiting my aunt Marika. She's a painter. She gave me a canvas and told me paint the jug of sunflowers on her windowsill. What I did looked like whirlwinds of mud."

"Painting," he said, picking a speck of tobacco from his lower lip. "Sunflowers." He shook his head. Then he rubbed his thumb on my nails until they took on a graphitic shine and all the paint was gone. Finally, he looked at my palm again. "Your love-line here—it's kind of twisted, you know." I doubted that he believed any such mumbo-jumbo. He asked, "Have you been engaged in some small anomaly?"

"What?" I wasn't sure of his French construction.

"Screwing, my little one. Who are you screwing?"

Michel was right, of course, in his question. My affairs in Paris had gotten non-linear. I was no longer sleeping with my Aunt Marika's lover, but that was because I was in love with my brother Thomas, and I had been sleeping with him for almost a year. It sounds flippant when I say it, but I don't mean it that way. It was a strange love, and in many ways blessed. Thomas had left the States when I was twelve and he was twenty-two; he had been in Paris for ten years, running his wine shop. Now I was learning about love from him, and also about wine. He was training me with those little bottles of fragrances that wine people use to help them describe the nose of a wine, those vials full of the smell of blackberries, limestone, new-mown hay.

I confided in Michel because he did not matter to me. With his hermit-like randiness, his aspect of a mad monk, I considered him not quite human; it was like airing my mind to a cat or a tree. As I tried to put things into words for Michel, I first began to think about that tangled forest we call love. It was as though, standing there in the semi-darkness describing my present, I became the teller of my future: I realized that when I spoke of love, I had to use the terms of light. To talk of Thomas was to call forth what the French call *L'Heure Bleue*, that bluest hour of twilight when the sky has a color so deep and sudden it makes your heart ache.

I didn't know, then, that all my future loves would correspond to some form of illumination. I do not mean that visible radiance which surrounds you when you are in love. The light I am talking of is hidden and peculiar, like a secret name. It doesn't describe the quality of the relationship, but arises from some particular condition: the low-slung orange moon when you first spend the whole night walking together; or the sun coming through the curtains when you first make love—though consummation is not necessary for this. Anyway, even twenty years later, Thomas is linked to the blueness of twilight. Michel can haunt me, even now, through certain cusps of light. Sitting outside on a sunny afternoon, I will find the "baby's bottom" cusp in my coffee cup, when there is just one swallow of liquid left: it looks like a heart without a point. The trefoil cusp tends to appear in restaurants at night, on a white table cloth, when I toy with my glass of wine. Any distant love can haunt you.

Of course, talking to Michel that first afternoon, I felt defensive, although he said almost nothing. I argued—I was quite strident at twenty-two—that love in any form was difficult; Thomas and I were two who made it work—why should it be denied to us? Our rare fights were no more vicious than those of ordinary couples. What did our friends think? The ones who could face the possibility simply accepted it; the ones who couldn't, refused to believe that we were lovers. Neither Thomas nor I was deluded into thinking it a permanent situation; we avoided talking about the future. I was a deeply un-introspective young woman, and it was only when trying to present it to Michel that I could see my affair with Thomas as though it were contained in a small vortex of time, finite, spiralling downstream.

As I spoke in the hazy dimness of Michel's laboratory warren, I paced within the confined space in front of his desk, while he toyed with a metal flange, twisting it with a pair of long-nosed pliers. When I was finally silent, he looked up at me and said with unusual softness, "Yes. I wondered if it was something like that."

"Something like what? What do you mean?"

"You seemed so abnormally taken up."

"Because I don't respond to you?" I didn't know how to react to his new gentleness.

"You know, you don't have to use that tone with me. Any more."

With Michel that day I had at last talked about Thomas

and suddenly felt what a burden it had been to keep silent.
Love wants to be mentioned, as though utterance makes it
more real. That year I had no intimate women friends; most
of my male friends were much closer to Thomas than to me,
and I could not talk to them about him. With Michel, it was
no longer like talking to an animal or a tree. People don't
stay trees for long. I stopped by to see him almost every day.
I began to linger in his room. He made coffee for me in an
odd contraption of glass spheres under vacuum. I would wash
the coffee cups in the black soapstone sink, though he assured me they were already clean. We sat there on wooden
swivel chairs, the occasional silences broken by the creaking
of the heavy springs. Sometimes I could get him to talk about
growing up in the south of France; he would tell me of his ex-
wife, a dancer, who lived in Avignon. He claimed to be
uninvolved for the moment, or rather, involved sexually but
not emotionally. At that time one could still do that. He said
he was Thomas's age, but I never knew for certain.

"And sex?" Michel asked, one afternoon.

"What do you mean?"

"How does it differ—with your brother?"

I didn't answer him then, but that night, lying beside
Thomas after making love, I had the disturbing realization
that I had been watching myself, in order to be able to describe it to Michel.

Michel had made me wonder if our love-making was in-
complete in some way, because we saw ourselves reflected in
each other. Not at all. The next afternoon I told Michel that
when I was in bed with Thomas, I sometimes looked at him
and thought, That's what my body would be like if I had been a

boy: that would have been my jaw, my chest, my penis. Though Thomas was lankier and full of shadows, still the same reddish glints were there. I felt it opened my perceptions and my senses to think of myself as partly my brother. I often wondered, though I never asked him, if Thomas felt the same.

Another day I slipped into Michel's room and watched him as he soldered tiny copper rings.

He took the ring he'd been working on and quenched it in a shot glass with a just audible hiss. Then, looking up at me, he said, "Coffee, is it? I seem to have lured you and now you are addicted. Go ahead, you may perform your cup-washing ritual. But is it for me, or the coffee, that you come here?"

I didn't answer, because at that point it wasn't either him or the coffee, it was having to explain myself that I found compelling.

"You look—not yourself. Are you OK?" Michel peered at me, as though he was inspecting me, in the way he did each afternoon. I wondered what he was looking for.

Then he asked, "When was your last period?"

This, coming out of the blue, surprised me. I hesitated and then said, "It will come."

"*Putain de merde.*"

"No, really it will. I'm often late." A slight spasm of doubt.

"Wait," He opened a drawer and took out a round shaving mirror. "Here, look at your face." He directed his desk lamp onto my face and I blinked for a moment in the glare.

"I don't see anything," I said. "What should I be seeing?"

"Learn to look at people. You can almost always tell when someone is in love, that is simple. But learn to see other conditions, as well. You, for example, are pregnant. Can't you see it? Can't you feel it?"

I shook my head. I was too bewildered to ask how he knew. I thought he was making some awful joke.

"Imbecile," he said, drawing out the syllables. Then, lowering his voice, "This is impossibly stupid of you. It's one thing to fuck your brother—any non-dead animal in the barnyard does that. But to omit the simplest precaution…"

"I didn't omit."

"Whatever you did, it was not sufficient. Go, tomorrow, get yourself tested."

I got up from my chair and went to the doorway and stood there with my back to him. I didn't go into the hallway because I was so close to tears I didn't want to be seen. When I could talk, I said, "Why are you being this way?" I didn't know what to make of his anger or his prediction.

He went to his workbench, where I could hear him pouring the coffee. He put his hand on my shoulder and led me back to my chair. "Here," he said. "Drink."

I looked at the coffee in my cup and it seemed abnormally black and thick. I wondered how one could drink such a substance. Again, Michel was inspecting me. I put my tongue to the liquid, like a cat.

The hospital was an old French fortress in the 15th *arrondissement*, grime-covered limestone, soot-colored slate, with towers at each corner of the central courtyard. They looked like the gun turrets of a prison. Thomas and I had wanted to go to the American Hospital, but Michel told us gruesome stories and convinced us that anywhere else in Paris would be better. Both Thomas and Michel came with me. In those days, even for procedures in the first trimester, the French kept you overnight. Thomas was silent as we walked through the courtyard to the Gynecological wing; Michel kept making small ironic comments, explaining French medical hierarchy. I realized that they were both more nervous than I was and tried to send them home once I was installed in my room, but they insisted on staying. Thomas said he knew a food shop in the neighborhood where he could buy dinner for the three of us. He left Michel with me.

Alone with Michel in my hospital room, I felt suddenly shy. The enforced non-privacy of even a private hospital room made me feel exposed, and the presence of the bed between us, as we sat in armchairs on either side of it, made it seem to loom there, as though the word "intimacy" were printed on the sheets in place of *"Hôpital Boucicault."*

Michel said, "I brought you some things." He opened his scarred leather briefcase and took out a towel, soap, a packet of Kleenex, toilet paper. "These are not provided by French hospitals. Americans are usually not aware of this." He was right; I hadn't known; I was so touched I didn't ask how he knew.

Thomas came back with dinner: two bottles of Bordeaux for the three of us, chilled artichokes, chicken with truffles in jelly, and an assortment of little cakes. Michel went down the hall and coaxed plates, glasses, silver, from the food service.

So we picnicked, me cross-legged on the bed, Thomas and Michel in armchairs, and we talked about everything but love and sex and siblings.

The abortion—which should have made me stop and think—did not. Perhaps it planted a seed of doubt or introspection, but I was not conscious of it then. In some way, I blamed Michel for my pregnancy, though I was not sleeping with him, because he had brought it to my attention and had directed such fury at me. I wondered often about that anger: whether it was caused by my thoughtlessness, my disregard for genetic outrage, my upsetting the pattern of our afternoons in his workroom, or simple worry.

Less than a week after the abortion, my mother—*our* mother—came from Boston to visit, though that was not why she came; she didn't know anything about it. Thomas and I moved all my clothes and books out of his place and into the empty apartment of one of his friends. There was a sadness to this move, this mimicking of departure, like the sadness that comes when you find yourself in tears chopping onions. As with certain types of fights, what starts as imitation can end up much too real.

The apartment was clearly too elegant for me, though it was sparsely furnished; I was sure my mother would see through it. She stayed in a small hotel that had once been an abbey; Thomas and I would pick her up and drive her around Paris in Thomas's seedy Rover sedan. She mostly wanted to go to museums. I have long had a horror of museums, and other conventionally silent places, such as libraries. When I was young, my mother would bring me to the art museum where she worked, sending me off to "explore and behave" while she did her research or gave lectures. I was terrible: I ran about, touched things, and refused to hush. The guards grew leery of me. I am better in museums, now, but I am still awful in libraries: I am possessed by wild giggles or an urgent need to talk.

Our mother asked us to take her to the Asiatic Museum on the Right Bank. The ancient temple at Borobudur in Java was being excavated and reconstructed, and a famous collection of sculpted heads had been brought to France for safekeeping. How I laughed to myself at her desire to see those heads. But Thomas and I accompanied her—anything to keep her from spending too much time inspecting my borrowed lodgings.

The museum had devoted several rooms to the large archaically smiling heads of Buddha. They were stunning. They silenced me. The rooms were completely dark except for spotlights on the massive puzzling and enticing stones. As Thomas and I wandered about with her, he kept a brotherly hand on my shoulder; I could tell he was as moved as I was by the heads, and as nervous about our situation.

Until yesterday I hadn't thought of those heads for twenty years. Megan's trip to Jakarta has reminded me that they are now reinstalled in central Java. When I leave here, I will probably go and see them. How we laugh at the passions of our parents, only to find ourselves sometimes afflicted by the same things. We repeat, as though latent genes are turned on. Thomas and I ridiculed our mother as we hid our own obsession from her. Only now does it occur to me to question whether she, too, was ever bothered by perverse loves.

The Sunday before our mother was to leave Paris for

Boston, Thomas gave a luncheon. I had helped him with the preparations that morning, and I stayed behind when he went to her hotel to pick her up. Aunt Marika, my mother's sister, came early with Stasek, a Polish photographer she was involved with. Stasek and I had also been lovers, earlier in the year, before I moved in with Thomas. I hoped Marika was still ignorant of this. At that lunch, I hoped everybody was ignorant of everything.

"Oh, how lovely," my mother said.

"Asparagus."

"Those tulips."

"More trout?"

The wine was golden yellow, scented with hay. I wanted to be outside, far from everyone.

"Cass, dear. There's something I haven't gotten a chance to ask you."

I couldn't look at anyone. I couldn't reach Thomas's foot under the table. I had wronged everybody at the table except him: Marika by sleeping with her lover, Stasek by going off with Thomas, Mother by sleeping with her son. Their faces loomed, distorted by my apprehension. The food in front of me was different forms of guilt, shaped as vegetables, shaped as fish.

"Are you looking a bit thin and pale, my dearest?"

"Studying, raining quite a lot." I knew I was incoherent, but I couldn't help it. Thomas carried in the roast beef. It was rare the way the French like it, bluish in the middle. Mother asked whether it was done enough. They discussed the meat while he stood there holding the platter. She agreed to taste it, and he agreed to cook it more if she didn't like it. I couldn't face any sort of flesh right then, and asked for just more bread and mustard. Mother said, "Oh, Cass. Protein." She changed the subject, "You know, I saw Marika's paintings, and she showed me the one she did of you. It's quite marvelous." I didn't know what to say to this. Marika had painted me in the nude one afternoon last May, when I was new in Paris and was still living at her apartment. All her friends and neighbors came in to watch. Stasek came, too. I hadn't met him before, but he sat beside me while I posed and we got into one of those startling subterranean conversations you can sometimes have, under the general hum of everyone else. The portrait, when I finally saw it, shocked me. I looked flayed, purple and green. The background was some kind of menacing forest, hallucinatory. I felt I was in that painting, now, though I was surrounded by lovers and family, at Sunday lunch. My shoulders ached; I realized that I had been pressing my arms against my ribs, as though to hold myself together.

"Cass, my love," my mother said. "You haven't told me of any of your recent boyfriends. I've never known you to be without one for long."

Save me, Thomas. Be a saint and save me. Say something. Spill your wine. Bring more food; something.

Thomas was silent, smiling, sure that I would come up with something. Stasek was smiling, indulgent; he had been wonderful to me, had taught me many things. Men always taught me things, that was why I loved them, for the way they charged through the world, figuring it all out. My mother and Marika looked at me, both of them red-haired and fair skinned, smiling, waiting. I stretched my leg under the table to see if I could touch Thomas's foot. He was too far away. "Well," I said, throwing myself into the vacuum formed by all the looks and smiles. "There is this guy at the lab." I began to describe Michel. I finally said, sheepishly, "I have to see him every afternoon or else my day doesn't make sense." This surprised me with its truth. I didn't say that we had never made love, never kissed, touched, never even talked of it, except in Michel's unserious way. Thomas got up from the table and put on a record of some persistent jazz.

"Turn it a bit lower, dear. Would you? I do so want to hear what Cass has been up to."

Perhaps I was annoyed at Thomas for not saving me; that may have led me to enhance my description. He puttered around, grinding coffee in the kitchen, clearing plates and stacking them noisily in the sink. I was upset, too; I under-stood, from listening to what I said, that I was in love with Michel. It seemed as though present words were influencing the past.

As soon as our mother went home to the States, I went over to Thomas's.

"Well, well," he said, when I let myself in. "I'm flattered that you could spare me the time from your beloved at the lab." He turned back to his wine catalogues, then added, "I hope you've already seen him today, we wouldn't want your day to lack meaning." I told him to cut it out. He asked how long it had been going on. I explained that Michel and I were not lovers, but we both knew that was irrelevant. Thomas opened one of his rarest wines, and we sat on the rug, our backs against the couch, fondly savoring the wine and its complexity—I claimed black currant and chocolate, he claimed blackberry and oak. I think we both felt lost and horrible as we tallied up the counts of our mutual betrayals. Mine, of course, were greater: falling for Michel clearly out-weighed silence in the face of our mother's question. We were both relieved that it was over. And terrified about how to proceed. We were still siblings, closer than ever, and full of sadness. It would have been most natural for us to spend the afternoon in bed, but sex was still forbidden to me so soon after the abortion.

I left Thomas's apartment, and moved out of his friend's place. I left physics and never looked back at it. I left the windowless rooms smelling of oil and solvents. Michel and I lived together for a few months, then I left Paris altogether. Since then, I have spent the past twenty years breeding plants—in Florida, Central America, Asia—clipping, pot-ting, grafting, all the fruitful gerunds of gardening, in green-houses and field stations, always under natural light.

That is what I tell Max our first night together.

The next morning we explore again on his motor bike. In the afternoon we sit outside and watch the sky as it changes from radiant, innocent blue to furious violet. When the rain comes, we move our wicker chairs back under the overhang-ing eaves. He teaches me to note the quality of rainlight, to see when the grey is more of a moss-green, as the rain is enveloping us, and when it is old bruises, as the storm moves off and we see the underside of the clouds. "I used to appreciate only forms of sunlight," he says. "But the light of the rainy season is interesting and strange." When the shower stops, we pull our chairs back to our former positions. We sit and talk. We argue about technology. He talks excitedly about his work in the museum here, putting slides of all their Chinese ceramics onto laser disc. I hate compact discs and video discs. Progress is never progress, I say.

"And the ancient Chinese potters—you don't think their glazes and ovens were the very latest?"

Mostly our arguing is a way of warding off the growing attraction between us. Of course, it doesn't work very well: one heat can easily fire up another. We don't talk about this and we don't act on it. Sometimes he will put his bare foot on my leg—I'm in long pants—but I read this only as some kind of restraining order, as saying, Don't move, don't leave, don't change anything.

Again, the night is hot. We talk outside until long after midnight, watching a pair of garden frogs follow each other across the grass and back.

In the guest room with louvered windows open to the call of tree frogs, I sleep naked. I presume he does too, in their room. I try not to think of it. All the windows are open, and the overhead fan turns silently, set at its slowest speed.

A storm comes at two in the morning. The vehemence of the rain leaves me gasping, as though in its forceful descent it has sucked away all the air. The rain is no longer particles but sheets, waves, volumes.

Even when the downpour has tapered off, the air is still

too breathless and electric to sleep. I put on a t-shirt and underpants and go down to the kitchen. Max sits there, in his shorts, drinking rum. "You too?" he asks. "Here, let me get you a glass." He fills my glass with ice and rum, then turns out the light. We sit at the kitchen table. The rain falls in single drops, now. He asks me why I'm not married. All my friends ask this, sooner or later. "Why have you never? Don't you think you should?" he asks. The real answer, of course, is that I don't know. It hasn't really been a conscious choice, rather that what I love about living alone—the silence, the lack of compromises—has always outweighed the promise of permanent company. I set my own schedule, I travel whenever I have money. I don't like to wait. "But," he says. "But."

"Of course," I reply, knowing, by now, all the objections.

"Plus, it's horribly selfish," he adds. At this point he places both his bare feet on top of mine, as we sit facing each other in the darkness. He is grounding me. He is also feeling selfish.

The first phone call comes then. He turns on the overhead fluorescent ring and we both grimace at the sudden light. It's 2:35. Megan, calling from Jakarta, is having a rough night. He talks her down. Long ago, I would do this for her—when we were in high school and she'd been up on something. Now, it's ordinary night-fears: she wonders how the children are, the younger one had a fever when she called Max's parents in the afternoon; the politics of international health is full of anguish; she gives her talk tomorrow. Max is wonderful with her, gentle and full of love, speaking as though it's never happened before. He gestures to me, to see if I want to speak to her. I put my finger to my lips. I don't want her to know I'm awake with him; my being in the house probably has more than a little to do with her fears, even though it was she who scheduled my visit. We have shared men before; she knows I am not a threat. I get up to tiptoe out of the room, thinking that Max might be more comfortable alone with her, but he catches my arm and steers me back to the table.

When the phone call is over, he refills our glasses with ice and rum.

"I used to do that," I say.

"I know," he says. "She told me." Then, "Hold on. I have to fix something." He goes into the living room and turns on a lamp, then comes back and switches off the kitchen light. For a while, neither of us says anything, as we get used to the new darkness, and the faint glow spreading from the other room.

"What about kids?" he asks.

"Yes, well. I'd make a terrible mother."

"Those who have doubts are the only ones fit to try it."

"Perhaps, but it's no guarantee."

"You're getting old, you know."

"Thanks."

"No, really. You should think about children."

"I have."

"No," he pauses. "I mean seriously."

From his tone, I begin to see what he is getting at. This is completely insane. "Do you mean..." I can't finish.

"Well, yes."

"But that's absurd. You don't even know me. You don't know how I'd be. Besides, you would want to participate, you would want some control, visits—without even being divorced or married." This is all happening too fast for me.

"I wouldn't interfere. I live here; you don't."

"You don't know how you'd feel; your desires would change."

"That is always possible."

"But why would you do this? What would you get from it?"

"Just knowing."

"Have you done something like this before?"

He looks at me sharply. "No. Never."

"Isn't it completely unthinkable?"

"Yes," he says. "But that doesn't mean you shouldn't think about it." He pauses, then says, " 'Unthinkable' has never stopped you before."

I get up and open the door to the garden. Standing on the threshold, I say, "That's pretty low."

"Sorry. I didn't mean it that way. I said it in admiration."

I walk outside. The rain has turned into powdery mist. The earth smells green and some flower I can't see is giving off its night fragrance. The fronds of the banana palm sway slightly, as though watching to see what will happen. Max follows me outside and stands behind me, his hands on my shoulders. I am torn between my immediate desire for him and anger at having to consider what he has proposed. His suggestion shimmers like an optical illusion flipping back and forth between possible and reprehensible. I simply want to sleep with him—something sweet and uncomplicated. I am about to tell him this when the phone rings again.

I stay out in the garden; I can hear him calming someone, but it doesn't seem to be Megan. "My mother," he tells me, when he hangs up. "One of the kids is sick. I'm sure it's her usual ear infection but I'd like to take her to the clinic. Would you come with me?"

We put on clothes and take Megan's car, this time, speeding through the rain-slicked empty streets. At Max's parents' house I stay in the car; soon he carries out his three year-old daughter, Sara, wrapped in a large terrycloth towel. She seems feverish and cries as I hold her.

There are no other patients in the emergency clinic; Sara and Max are seen right away. Though she is still whimpering as we leave, she falls asleep in my arms during the drive home. As Max carries her into the house she wakes again and frets. He talks soothing nonsense to her, then turns to me, asking if I would make us something to drink and bring it upstairs. In the kitchen, I add orange juice to the rum and ice, thinking that it will soon be morning.

In the bedroom, Sara lies between us, sleeping calmly. We talk, watching the shadows of the ordinary things on the dresser in the glow of a single candle. The mood between us is tender and knowing—as if we were beyond courtship, though we are not, we are just exhausted. Later today, Sara will return to her grandparents' house. Max and I will be alone again with our arguments and possibilities. I will think, then, about what to do.

The windows and shades are open; the sky has that hesitation of just before dawn.

In the Garden

A S SOON AS HIS GUESTS LEFT, MARTIN HURRIED TO THE GREEN-
house to bring the plants into the living room. As he
went, he took off his dinner jacket and tie and dropped them on
the front hall table. Unbuttoning the top stud of his shirt, he
shooed away the tabby cat who tried to rub against his legs.

The larger trees towered over him, but their green wooden
tubs rolled easily on casters. They clattered loudly as he pushed
them, one by one, over the stone tiles of the hall. Upstairs,
Hillie, his new wife, shifted in her sleep, smiled briefly, and
went on dreaming.

Two orange trees he placed just at the edge of the red orien-
tal carpet, forming a gateway into the rest of the room. His
glasses had steamed up and as he polished them with his hand-
kerchief he looked around nearsightedly. He liked to start with
the larger trees; they made a framework for the rest. The banana
trees were on rollers, also the palms with their long fringes, and
the various species of bamboo: the *Sinobambusa* with its purplish
stalks, and the giant *Dendrocalamus*. He didn't move them about

often, only when he'd been drinking a fair amount and talking with his friends about the old days.

⌒

It was unusually warm for the south of England, and as he unlatched the windows to let in the damp midnight air, he unbuttoned the rest of his shirt. Already the living room smelled less of stale cordials and cigar ash, as the orange trees, jostled by the move, gave off their fragrance.

Martin worked slowly, pausing sometimes to run his fingers down the central spine of a palm leaf, feeling its resilience. He knew that this arrangement would take the better part of the night. It wasn't totally accurate: there hadn't been any fig trees behind his cabin in Lower Burma, but he liked the texture they gave to the scene, so he pushed them in anyway. Also he hadn't succeeded with tropical Asian fruits here in Britain: the mangosteens and rambutans refused to sprout, the durians sent up etiolated stalks which dwindled and died.

He hugged the pots of jasmines close to him as he carried them in, the white ones with their maddening sweetness, the yellow ones tickling his neck and swaying over his shoulder, lithe and tipsy like young girls at the end of the dance.

His view camera stood on its tripod by the couch, its black cape ruffled on top of the teak wood box. He didn't think he would use it tonight, but he felt comfortable having it there—a friendly presence—and he wouldn't have to explain himself if anyone should happen in on him.

It wasn't likely that anyone would. Hillie had excused herself before the brandy. She was in the early months of pregnancy and tired easily.

They had met in London while she was finishing some research and translation for one of his colleagues. Martin had offered her a job editing his book, *Plant Forms of Lower Burma*. He was pleased by how quickly she fell in with his project and made his dreams her own. When she told him he ought to marry again, he had proposed on the spot. She was sweet, bright and fertile. She caught on quickly.

He had been alone for two years after coming back to England. He supposed it would be good for him to have a family; Hillie told him it would.

Upstairs Hillie tossed in her sleep. She enjoyed giving dinners, although it made her uneasy when the talk narrowed down to Rangoon and Moulmein after the war.

Martin had left Burma a couple of months after the violent disappearance of Gwen, his first wife. He hadn't wanted to leave, hadn't thought he could bear to quit the jungle and his primitive photo lab. The Forest Administration boys had pushed him, saying he should rest up in England, then come out again when the fever was gone. Perhaps if Maung Ho had stayed, he could have wrapped himself in his mosquito net and cured himself there, in his hut. But Maung Ho had family business to attend to, and had gone to the north.

Lovely Gwen. She'd photographed people rather than vegetation. She spent her days in the villages, happiest when in the thick of faces and talk. He felt partitioned off, except among the plants.

∾

Hillie did not know what Martin did when he stayed up late on summer nights. She did not feel she knew him well at all, but this did not upset her. In some way she had married him not to find out. Coming from a family with too many siblings and too many desires, she found a haven in Martin's silence.

Hillie had left the north of England to go to university in London, where she found she had an amazing love of, and gift for, languages. When she realized that there was nothing God-given about the music of English, she found it simple to grasp the rhythm of any new language and internalize it, humming its music to herself until she was ready to pin meaning onto it. She took jobs interpreting and translating, finally moving down to Dorset to work with Martin. And fall in love with him. He echoed her thoughts when he put his arms around her, saying, "I am so lucky to have found you."

All she really knew of him after four months of marriage was his gentleness and the way he visited his greenhouse before breakfast, caressing the leaves, looking for new bloom.

That morning, with a thin mist rising from the garden in the unusual heat, they had thrown open the windows of the morning room before they sat down. The shimmer of yellow sunlight on the terrace made the caged parrots exclaim loudly. Wild finches chattered back from the shrubbery. Hillie poured tea.

"Shall I send them off then, the proofs?" she asked. Martin's book was finally completed.

"Yes. It's time they got off."

"Perfect timing, then. The dinner tonight will be a celebration." She stirred her tea, saying, "I wish we'd thought to have music as well. We haven't danced since the wedding, and I loved doing it with you. Tell me we'll do it soon."

He blew her an agreeing kiss and she grinned in return.

Spreading a piece of toast with butter and a thick layer of marmalade, she handed it to him. "Does it make you sad, sending it in for good?"

"A bit. Yes. A lot, actually. I suppose it's a farewell to the jungle."

She took his hand and put it to her cheek, as though the warmth and smoothness there would help him. Then she kissed his palm and closed his fingers over it.

"And the dedication?" She asked. "They're asking what you've decided to do. Will it be to Gwen?"

"Would that be all right, then?" He looked down at his hands, opening the one she had kissed, then closing it quickly.

"Of course, my love," she said warmly. "She was your wife. You dedicate it to Gwen, and you can put Maung Ho in the acknowledgments. And also me."

During their courtship, Martin had shown Hillie pictures of the house at the edge of the jungle where he had lived for ten years. His pale blue eyes lit up as he presented his photographic portraits of tropical plants and flowers. He polished a magnifying lens and handed it to her while he pointed out details. He lingered over descriptions of male and female flowers and exotic fruits.

"It grows a good twenty feet high," he said, giving her a picture of a mangosteen tree. "The leaves are large ovals—they glisten in the sun. And the skin of the fruit is a deep purplish brown. But the flesh is a creamy translucence—oh God, and it tastes like everything you could ever want. I haven't been able to get it to grow in England, even in the greenhouse. Otherwise, I would grow one for you." Then he kissed her.

There was only one photograph of Gwen, her cropped red hair and green eyes appearing weak and faded in the black and white.

"But surely you have more pictures of her?" Hillie asked.

"I had her beside me," Martin explained. "I didn't think to observe her. Besides, she would threaten to turn her camera on me. She would go after the villagers, you know, and photograph them. I could never do that; it makes me nervous to take pictures of people. But she liked it. That was her job, writing about them, photographing them, and sending it all back to the newspapers here. She would talk to them, and even bring a few home, sometimes. She felt quite close to Maung Ho, our neighbor. Extraordinary fellow. Studied at mission schools, then got sent to Rangoon on a fellowship. He worked for almost a year in the city, at an administrative job, but couldn't stand it. So he quit and came back to the jungle, getting odd jobs as a tracker. Worked for us as a guide and lived in a hut next door. Wonderful specimen. Very upset when Gwen died."

Martin stopped himself and went to his closet, bringing Hillie another white cardboard box of photos. He undid the string around it and handed her the first picture. It showed Gwen's blouse, light-colored with blackish streaks of blood. The shirt lay stretched flat on the earth. A small rock held down each sleeve at the wrist.

"Oh my God," Hillie burst out. "But why…?"

"It was all I had left," he said. "There was a breeze; I had to put the rocks there to keep it from flapping about. It would not hold still."

There was another view of the front of the shirt, from a different angle, and two pictures of the back, again with rocks on the sleeves and now smaller stones at the collar and along the bottom. The wind must have come up as he worked.

"It was green, the shirt. She always wore it."

Speechless, Hillie hugged him, wanting to protect him from his loss. She thought of suggesting he bury the pictures, but in the end decided to keep silent.

"I think I was much better out there, until this happened." He paused. "I'm not good with people, you know," he said, finally. "I don't know how to talk about the ordinary things. Can you perhaps bear with me?"

She held him close.

Hillie never told Martin that the story of his first wife's death was not totally believable.

Martin had not been there when Gwen died. He had gone to Moulmein to pick up a shipment of film and chemicals. The morning that he left, Maung Ho had come over to warn them about tigers. Man-eaters, he said. An epidemic of pox was ravaging a distant village. There had been no time for proper burial ceremonies. Instead, the remaining villagers threw the bodies into a ravine.

"Tigers came to eat the bodies," Maung Ho said. "And so now they have the taste for human flesh. Not like before, when they had respect. I have seen tiger prints in the morning in the dirt around my fire; he has come to see me while I sleep. Come to look. And then go away, because he respects me: I am hunter, he is also hunter. That was before; not like now." A village girl had been mauled and carried off the day before, he said, while she was harvesting corn.

Martin had tried to extract a promise from Gwen that she would not be foolish. When he had come back from the city, she was gone.

After three days, Maung Ho came and stood weeping in the doorway, holding Gwen's green shirt. Martin broke down.

"Is that all? Nothing else?"

He gathered his gun and water pouch and went off with Maung Ho into the jungle. For a week they hunted spoor; Martin following blindly the path hacked through the undergrowth by his guide. They came upon carcasses, hideous in the heat, but each time Maung Ho said they were not human remains. She was not there. Maung Ho wanted to stop and fish in the deep pools of a stream, using small fruits as lures, but Martin pressed them on, saying they could live on the rice they carried.

Feverish and starving, they finally gave up and went home. Martin stayed in his hut, in bed, while Maung Ho set out with a band of his friends to search more.

After four days, Maung Ho appeared with Gwen's camera. He told where he had found it, under a fruit tree, with no signs of struggle or prints. He had lost one of his men.

"We were sitting in the jungle, gambling, around the fire."

"How do you mean, 'gambling'?"

"You cut two tamarind seeds in half, so you have one white side and one black. Then you shake them in a bamboo cup, it makes a noise: *kak kak kak kak*. And while you shake, everyone bets. Po Mya was shaking, and everybody sat quiet, concentrating on the color. *Kak kak kak kak*, no other noise. One thing, like lightning, came and grabbed him because he was the only thing moving. Everybody else was sitting like stumps of trees."

"Lightning came?" Martin had not yet understood Maung Ho's story.

"No lightning," Maung Ho moaned. "Tiger. Like lightning. Very quick, you know. Very quick a tiger came and grabbed Po Mya because he was shaking tamarind seed *kak kak kak kak* in the cup. Other people all sitting still. The tiger not sure they are alive. All may be stumps of trees. But he is one hundred percent sure Po Mya live human, so he grabbed that man."

"How can this be true?"

"Oh, yes. Witnesses. Many people left to tell about this story. One man, he says: 'That is ghost'—You know ghost?—Come to take Po Mya away. Come so quickly. Other man says: 'That is God who come to take him'. So fast he was, that tiger. One man say: 'Yellow tiger'. I say: 'White tiger'. Because I don't know. Very quick."

Maung Ho led Martin to the spot in the jungle where this had happened. Signs of a campfire, a scuffle, tracks of a cat.

The village headman called for a hunt. Martin was too sick to leave his hut. He had lost hope that Gwen was still alive and was afraid of what they would find. He was sick at heart; the jungle he so loved had betrayed him.

Maung Ho brought him the details. The tiger had been spotted around the village even by day. He was an old tiger with a peculiarly stubby tail.

"So old, old tiger, he came and roared all around the village, very strong: 'AAHHM, AAHHM. I want to eat. I want to mate.' Oh, everyone was shaking.

"In the morning, the head of the village hurried very many hunters to make a cage. Bamboo poles thick as my arm, stuck in the soil. Two hunters stay in the cage, with rifles. But they shoot too early, before the tiger comes out of jungle. Failure."

Hillie had watched Martin's eyes as he told her these stories. He did not show any signs of doubt. As she handed back to him the black and white pictures, she couldn't help noticing that the shirt was not torn, front or back, but she did not comment. This was Martin's story and she didn't want to press him to tell it differently.

"Was it a white tiger, then?" Hillie asked. "Did you finally see it?"

"I never saw it. I never saw any tigers at all."

The last few plants wouldn't fit in the living room; Martin placed them in the hall. He took his discarded shirt and wiped the sweat from his face and neck.

He unlocked a mahogany desk at the side of the room and withdrew a box of small brass bells and a spool of fine string. This he began to weave among the plants in the hall. Keeping the string at a foot's height from the floor, he tied bells to it—making a trip wire to alert him if anyone should come into the hall.

The tinkling of the bells, as he secured them in place,

woke a pair of striped cats who had been asleep on the cool stone floor by the windows. They came to nudge and nuzzle him while he worked. They were Gwen's cats; all the cats had been hers.

When all the strings were in place, Martin went to the morning room and took down the bird cages, leaving the black covers on to keep them quiet. In the living room, he latched all the windows, and took out the small parrots, green with dashes of yellow. Cupping them in his hands to calm them, he whispered as he placed them in the branches of the hothouse plants. They woke, chirping and muttering, and hopped from branch to branch, watching him with quizzical tilted looks.

More household cats—they were all tabbies, Gwen had liked tabbies—hearing and smelling the uncaged birds began to slink in among the pots.

He had brought his rifle back with him from Burma; he felt it would be expected of him, though he had never used it except to make sure it fired. Loading it with cartridges from his desk, he laid his cheek against the cool of the barrel. It smelled of the sweet sharpness of gun oil. One of the parrots called out.

Martin said, "Shh, pretty one, don't worry."

He went around the room and turned out the lights. The night sky was pearling into dawn. Crawling in among the plants with his rifle beside him he lay down on his back. He took off his glasses and the leaves and birds grew larger, wilder. The ruby-colored earth of the carpet smelled of mold and night-blooming jasmine. The birds hopped from branch to branch, taking forays onto bookcases and curtain rods, but always flying back to the greenery. They cackled now at the cats who stalked them.

∞

The heavy, almost tropical air pressed down on her and Hillie couldn't sleep. She flung her arm out, feeling for Martin, but not finding him. He probably hadn't been able to sleep either and hadn't wanted to wake her. He often kept late hours, sometimes photographing a plant or two in the living room. As she sat up, she felt something inside her, fleeting, like the brush of a butterfly's wing. She stiffened, waiting for it to happen again. It wouldn't be real unless it repeated. She placed both hands lightly on her belly and kept still, only turning her head to read the clock. Half past four. It came again, whisk—whisk. She leaned back and smiled. She wanted to call it out, to announce it to him.

In the bathroom, she splashed her face with cold water and ran a brush through her short blond hair. She checked her naked body in the mirror for any other miracles, and thought that maybe her belly was rounder, her breasts not quite so small. Turning sideways she swayed her back, pushing her abdomen out to look the way she thought it should. There, it came again, just a quick flicker of sensation. "I've woken it up," she thought, smiling.

In the bedroom, she threw on her nightgown, pale green lace—she had brought it with her for the wedding—and hurried out to look for Martin.

Finding his study dark, she raced down the corridor connecting the east wing to the rest of the house. Still smiling, she thought of the effect this news would have on him. He had been uncertain about having children. She had assured him it would be wonderful and now she had proof that it was.

A gunshot cracked as Hillie came down the wide curved staircase. Then another. Parrots flew towards her, squawking, beating their way up the stairwell to perch on the chandelier. Potted plants stood clustered in the hall. The living room was a forest. A ringing of small bells. She started to trip over a string and caught herself.

Everything looked wrong, upside-down. Trees packed into the living room. Martin lying under them half-naked, streaked with dirt.

"Martin? Oh God, are you all right?" A fall, a stroke, she thought. An intruder. Make him be all right. Too many plants here. She couldn't really see. His gun. He's been shot. "Speak, love. Tell me. What is it?"

The orange cat lay sprawled, bleeding onto the dirt beneath a palm tree. Hillie shuddered, suddenly cold. She just wanted Martin to be alive. Then, anything else she could manage, they could manage together. Something inexplicable in the jungle.

"I shot the cat," he said thickly. He propped himself up on one elbow.

"I know," she said.

She slipped in among the plants.

"What are you doing?" he asked.

She lay down next to him. "I can't see from out there. I want to see what it looks like from where you are."

Beside her Martin lay back exhausted and closed his eyes. She saw now that the black marks on his skin were mixed with green, mold from the plant pots. He looked peaceful, as though after a great exertion.

Overhead, the palm leaves filtered the early morning light.

Flowering vines and banana fronds blocked her view of the front hall. The orange trees seemed very far away.

Hillie got up slowly and went over to the windows, pulling each of them wide open.

"Where are you going?" he asked.

"I think we should get it out of here," she said. "I think we should bury it before any of the servants get up."

She picked up the dead cat. It weighed more than she expected and she had to hold it against her breasts. Martin came to her.

"Look here, don't you want me to carry it? You'll get yourself all bloody."

"I've got it now. Could you bring your shirt?"

They found a shovel in the garden shed and buried the animal in the black loam underneath the rhododendrons. Then she asked him to dig a smaller hole beside it. Pulling her blood-streaked nightgown over her head, she folded it and laid it in the dirt.

Standing naked in front of the bushes, she stretched her arms above her, saluting the morning. Then she took his white shirt and put it on. He looked at her, radiant in the opalescent light. There was a smear of blood on the pale skin between her breasts. He rubbed softly at the stain with his thumb, wanting to kiss her breasts and the faint mark between them. Instead he closed the shirt, smoothing the pleats, and slowly buttoned it.

He pulled her to him, humming a slow waltz. They began their long and complex dance, twined around each other, turning slowly across the dew-covered grass. The first rays of golden sun lit now the skin of his bare chest, now her naked thighs.

Presences

KATE HESITATES AT THE DOORWAY OF THE HOSPITAL ROOM LOOK-
ing to see if Joey is awake. Joey's bandages are off, and
her shaven skull is neatly seamed with stitches. As she opens
her eyes to look at Kate, Joey's face is pale and luminous and
knowing. "Hi," she says. "How's my wise older sister?" Her
words come out bright and slowed. Kate likes the term *wise*
and grins whenever Joey says it, though she knows it is because she is a biologist and is the only one in the family who
can explain medical terms. Kate makes Joey understand the
size of things—a gram, a milligram, an X-ray. She tells her
how cells behave when they are acting badly. She provides
the names for the symptoms which haunt her sister.

"I'm late, my beautiful one, I know," Kate says, leaning
over to kiss her sister. She feathers one palm across Joey's
cheek, and Joey places her own hand on top of it pressing it
there, for a moment, harder.

Kate removes her coat to show off her dress. When Joey
went into the hospital Kate bought herself clothes; now she

tries to vary her appearance as much as possible for each afternoon's visit. In the rest of her life, she wears jeans and t-shirts, but she hopes that dresses can add an element of cheerfulness, or even humor, since she always feels somewhat foolish in a dress, even in an ordinary print like this one with its old-fashioned, pink and cream flowers—probably hydrangeas—on a blue background. As she turns around to show the pattern of the fabric, she feels strong inside her tall body and awkward because of her health. She starts to explain her lateness, saying, "I've got squirrels in the attic again."

"Yeah," Joey says. "Me too."

Kate doesn't know how to take this. She feels she should allow Joey to talk any way she wants, but it makes her uneasy when Joey is not down to earth. Metaphor points the way to gloom, Kate thinks. So she asks if Joey's husband has been taking care of the squirrels.

"No, dummy. How can he? They're my squirrels. Up here." Joey taps the top of her head, lightly.

Kate says, "No you don't. They told us they got essentially everything out."

"Then why am I like this?" Joey makes a sweeping gesture with her left hand and the IV lines follow. She is asking why she is back in the hospital, after surgery, which was supposed to be minimal this time. There had been wild brain hemorrhaging and a brief coma, followed by six weeks of learning to walk again and of figuring out where the words for things were hiding. Finally, Joey had been well enough to go home, but stayed only a week; it got too scary for the others to have her there; she was losing everything she had regained. Now she is given tests, to which there don't seem to be answers: her surgeons have contradictory explanations, and nothing seems to converge.

"Why you're like this is—pressure, probably," says Kate, earnestly parroting the theory of one of the surgeons. "Fluid, up there. They can drain it, or put in a shunt, and you'll snap back into place."

"I'm not so sure."

Kate isn't sure either. She suddenly doesn't want them to touch Joey again. She used to be certain that Joey would pull through on sheer force, and Joey had confided in her how much she needed her sister's optimism. What Kate hadn't told her was that it had been ignorance, not hopefulness: she hadn't read the booklets from the Cancer Society, which Joey had sent away for. When she did finally read their stark probabilities, Kate felt bleak and crumpled, unable to put on a show. Then Joey was given an experimental treatment—a string of tiny radioactive beads implanted where the tumor had been. Kate knows that this makes all the old statistics irrelevant, invalid, so she has been hopeful again, and tries to appear more so.

"Joey," she says, trying to change the subject. "I learn so much from you."

"You mean how to do all this?" She gestures toward the walls of the room, then points to tubes and machines.

"No. I just think you're extraordinary."

"Well if I'm so wonderful, why is Mom so pissed at me?"

"Mom?"

"Yeah. She said she's furious at my hair-do."

Because their mother has been dead for eleven years, Kate doesn't know what to say. She blushes a fierce red and peers at her sister to see how to read her, to see if it is just Joey's normal impishness. "Mom?" she asks again.

Joey looks straight back at her, serious and alert. "Yes, she was here, and she said she doesn't like the way I've done my hair." She smiles, shaking her head slowly. "Can you imagine, we're still arguing about hair, after all this time." She touches her free hand to her shaven skull, rubbing her fingers over the track of stitches. "And I don't even have any."

Kate watches her, trying to keep the surprise out of her face. "I see," she says calmly, afraid that Joey will turn skittish and not tell her anything if she reacts too strongly or points out too soon that their mother has been dead for more than a decade. As a demonstration of her unconcern she gets up smoothly from her armchair and walks to the window where she busies herself with the cards and flowers. She doesn't want to look at Joey any more; instead she reads the letters which have come, props up the cards that have fallen over, marvels at the exotic bouquets now offered by commercial florists: Holland bulbs in miniature spring forests, orchids like yellow jade. Plucking out wilted blossoms and dried stalks, then taking each arrangement to the sink to water it, she hopes Joey will see what she is doing as an attempt to make ordered beauty of those parts that are still alive; she hopes this because she realizes, after she has started working with the plants, that there is a brutal alternative reading: when things are gone by, we dump them out.

When Kate had learned their mother was dying, her immediate, gut-stabbing, reaction was: what will become of the garden? Their father, though he nursed their mother valiantly and with infinite sweetness, had no real sense for gardens; he was better at gathering brush in the forest. Their mother died at home, her bed strewn with books on Asian art. She was jaundiced from liver cancer, and looked ancient and quintessential when she died, appearing somehow Egyptian or Chinese. In the end, no one really took care of that garden; different friends came and planted day-lilies in odd places. A Rose of Sharon tree, a plant their mother had never liked, appeared in the middle of the upper lawn. No one could remember having ordered it.

Showering Joey's plants in the sink, Kate doesn't know what to say. This is the first time Joey has been mistaken about facts. She doesn't look unsure or disoriented, nor is there any sign of her normal mischievousness. Kate wishes Joey hadn't said that their mother visited her. She wants it so badly that she plays over the afternoon in her mind, leading up to her first moment in the doorway, as though by replaying she can make things take a different path. Perhaps if she had been on time, she thinks, and hadn't bothered about the squirrels.

There is another moment Kate has been reworking, a Valentine's Day party at the house of a mutual friend, a poet. It is a year and a half earlier and Joey is still well. Kate and Joey are in the dining room. Kate's husband is talking to a short round poet and Kate strains to hear what they are saying as she also tries to converse with Joey who has come alone because her husband is home with flu. Thumping music plays in another room.

"It's a pity they aren't dancing, yet," says Joey. "Though I always wonder what the poets are thinking about when they dance."

The early guests have clustered by the food in the dining room. A tall black woman with the posture of an administrator is saying, "Look, I appreciated my trip to China, I really appreciated it. But I have to admit, there was simply no Epiphany."

Kate watches Joey's gaze as it travels around the room and is suddenly afraid she is boring her sister with her description of the biological essay she is writing, about ripple patterns in fingerprints and zebra skins. Such inattention is odd, the sisters usually having too much, rather than too little, to talk about.

"How is the novel going?" Kate asks.

"Slow," Joey says, her eyes looking now at the door to the kitchen. Kate glances behind her and ascertains that there is no one there—the door is open just a slit. She can't see why her sister is gazing at it and wonders if Joey is depressed; she sets out to cheer her by telling a little story of daily life.

Joey is not listening any more; she stares so intensely at the kitchen door that Kate is spooked and again turns to look. Nothing. Kate has decided that her conversation has put her sister in a desultory mood; she wonders why she can't spark a connection in that warm and immediate way that is usual for them. She keeps talking, seeking the words and the topic that will make her sister come back, trying not to ask herself if Joey is being a little rude in not even pretending to listen. Joey takes on a bit of a scampish grin as she begins to throw her arms about in a sort of dance. At first, it is a beautiful spiral motion and Kate feels a pang of habitual jealousy: ever since both women were teenagers, Joey has always been an amazing dancer. Now, though, Joey's cup of grapefruit juice has flown out of her hand, and her arms jerk about in an ungainly mockery of dance, her eyes still turned to the left as though seeking the door. Kate is momentarily embarrassed at the strangeness of this flailing and catches at her sister's wrist trying to slow her down, to steady her until she finds her own control, but Joey is taller than she is, and more muscular, and the seizure is stronger than either of them. Joey spins, moaning and grabbing at the air and though Kate is still gripping her wrist, she cannot prevent her sister from falling heavily against the edge of the wooden table and collapsing on the floor. Joey's face is purple, froth escapes the corners of her mouth and she makes strange noises of breathing through clenched teeth. Kate thinks, Oh Lord, in front of all these people, I hope they're not upset or embarrassed by this. She thinks, What a dumb reaction.

Through the subsequent course of her sister's brain cancer, Kate replays that Valentine's party to the point of the lagging conversation, always arriving at the conclusion that if she had been able to keep her sister's attention, there would have been no disease.

Now, in Joey's room, as Kate picks at the flower arrangements, plucking off browned azalea blossoms, pulling out miniature white orchids that have wilted, she re-imagines walking into Joey's room, again and again, up to the point where Joey mentions their dead mother's visit.

"Listen," Kate says. She wants to do all the talking, partly to keep Joey from telling her any more, partly because she still needs Joey's advice. "You've got to help me figure out what my girls are up to." Kate's fourteen-year-old twins are in their first year of high school. They're not identical to each other, and they seem unlike anyone Kate knows. She thinks being a twin is probably awfully difficult, and suspects hers are stranger than most. "I went down to the cellar this morning, the main drain is in trouble again. The plumber was about to come and I wanted to make sure he could get at it, because there's usually parts of old brass beds stored there, and other stuff." Kate is pacing by the foot of Joey's bed. "Well, I found this thing; this... altar. It had a couple of human leg bones laid out on it and a horse hoof, and candles all over the place, some in candlesticks from the dining room." Kate looks into the hallway where a nurse is hurrying away, then turns back to Joey. "There was a skeletal falcon gripping a branch, it's all bones except for ruffs of feathers around the ankles; and a lace tablecloth, and a bowl of oranges. And a syringe, big enough for a horse." Kate goes to the window again and perches on the ledge among the flowers and cards. "What do you make of it, Joey?" Even though Joey's own daughters are younger, still in middle school, Kate often asks her what to do.

"Where did they get all that stuff, anyway?"

"I know where the bones come from," Kate says, getting up and shaking out her dress; she wants some violent exercise, feels caged. "The bones were on a table of discards outside one of the teaching rooms in the biology labs." Kate stops and gestures with both arms, then wonders why she has to be so dramatic. "Oh, God," she says. "I encouraged them. I told them to take the bird, too. And an unidentified fish. I thought it would make them inquisitive about something besides hair and boys." She turns to the sink and dampens a paper towel, then starts to wipe fallen blossoms and greenish-yellow pollen from the window ledge. "So I had to hide all that stuff, before the plumber came to fix the drain."

Joey cocks her head at her sister, and says with a bit of a smile, "I can see you wanting to get rid of it all for the plumber, but why does it worry you so? It's just bones."

"And syringes and candles, and tablecloths."

"Probably a project of some sort."

Kate is out of breath. "Listen," she says, "Am I exhausting you? Why don't I get you some cranberry juice or something? Ice? I'll get myself some coffee and I'll come right back. OK?"

As she passes the nursing station, Kate stops to talk to the staff; they know her by now. She chats a moment with Yevgeni, a burly laughing-eyed nursing assistant, new to Boston from Moscow, who keeps a paperback book beside him. Its cover is hidden by a page of lace underwear cut from the Victoria's Secret catalogue, neatly taped like a child's schoolbook. Kate has always wondered what Yevgeni's book is. Today it is open, and she can finally see that what he has been hiding is a Russian-English dictionary. As Yevgeni talks to her, he keeps his pudgy forefinger on a word.

"Your sister, today, is wanting to sit beside window? You shall tell me, I shall carry her to chair. I shall carry her to…" He looks down at his page. "To anywhere."

"I'll tell you," Kate says.

When Kate returns with their drinks, Joey asks her, "So what did you do with the bones and the candles?"

"I stuffed them all in that little closet off my darkroom. I got it out of the way before the plumbers tramped in with their pickaxes. Of course I missed a bone, a femur. When no one was looking I kicked it behind the furnace."

"So what do the twins say about it all?"

"Oh, dear. Do I have to ask them? You don't think I can let it just blow over?"

"What does Daniel say about it?"

"Men worry so. You know how fragile they are. I'd rather tell him after I know what it is."

"Well, you have to ask the girls, then," Joey says. "Come on, how bad could it be, anyway?"

A Food Services aide, dressed in pink with a pink hair net, knocks on the door and carries in Joey's dinner. Kate angles the rolling tray-stand over the bed. The afternoon nurse comes in to check Joey's vital signs and leaves her a miniature paper cup containing seven pills.

When the nurse retreats, Joey turns to Kate with a mischievous grin, holding up a pill and saying, "See this long white one? With the red stripe? He's a Chinaman and he's swooning with love for Joey. He's suicidal, he stands on the edge of the Yellow River where it flows east across Inner Mongolia, the great slow sloppy Yellow River which looks surprisingly like… chicken soup. See, he throws himself in, calling, 'Joey, I love you.' He knows that Joey will eat him." She drops her anti-seizure medication into the plastic bowl of soup. "He's drowning among the noodles, but Joey will save him, sort of." She spoons noodles, soup and pill into her mouth, then grimaces and swallows. She continues: "Now we have a little red one. He has high blood pressure, and maybe a bit of a limp. He's going mountain climbing anyway, high among the crystal crags of berry-flavored Jello." She slides the red pill into a cleft in the Jello.

"Aren't you going to eat it?" Kate asks. She's not frightened by this, she thinks Joey knows what she's doing. Antics are needed because otherwise Joey cannot get herself to take pills; she has always tended to gag on them.

"No, not yet. He wants to experience the solitude of the high mountains a bit, to be alone in the quivering stillness. Meanwhile, we have the muddy-green stool softener. He's always been an explorer in the swampy jungles south of the equator and right now he's yearning for this puddle of creamed spinach."

Watching Joey poke the green pill into the spinach and then take random forkfuls, Kate asks, "Did you get it?"

"I think so. Not so sure, though." Joey tilts her head and grins. "Now the white ones, here, go into the mashed potatoes. They've been known to languish there for hours." She lines up four white pills of various sizes on the edge of her plate and flicks them with her middle finger toward the mashed potatoes and the slab of grey-brown meat. The last pill rolls onto the floor. "Three out of four into the potatoes, that's pretty good," Joey says.

Kate gets on her hands and knees to find the getaway pill. "What kind was it, do you know? Should we call the nurse?"

"Don't worry about it. They always bring more. Really, Katie, one or two pills, here or there—it doesn't actually matter, you know."

Kate stops looking for the pill and sits down again.

"You know," Joey says. "Mom shouldn't really be pissed at my hair. Her head is shaven now, too."

"Why?" Kate asks; she breathes in and out, slowly, then asks, "Has she had a brain tumor, too?"

"Oh yes. She's on the next floor up, didn't you know? She looks just the same as me."

"What about Dad?" Kate says, keeping her words even and light-sounding. Their father has been dead for seven years. "Does he visit?"

"Not so often. He doesn't interfere so much. He never did. But Etta comes, bossy as ever. I just can't seem to get away from that woman, even though she lives in Paris." Etta, Joey's mother-in-law, was buried in Père Lachaise Cemetery four years earlier.

Kate knows she will have to disabuse Joey about these people; she feels she ought to anchor her sister in reality if she can. It's hard enough to be in the floating hell of hospital life without having people skirt around the truth. She can't bring herself to start, and asks instead, "What does Etta say to you?"

"Mostly she talks about what I'm eating. She doesn't think IV's are a good idea. She doesn't think I should eat the meat, here. She wants me to eat more carrots."

When their mother was dying of liver cancer, Etta visited the United States. Their mother was already yellow from the lack of liver function and if she ate anything at all it was green Jello; she kept asking for "the fruit whose name begins with the letters 'th'." Kate and Joey couldn't figure out what she meant. Etta, never a good listener, went shopping and brought back two bushel-baskets of organic carrots. By the time Kate and Joey figured out that their mother had really meant 'papaya,' she was no longer eating anything at all. The rest of the family worked on the carrots.

"Look," Kate says to Joey. "Do you want to get up and sit in the armchair for a while? Yevgeni said he would carry you."

"Oh, no. I couldn't possibly sit up," Joey says, drawing her hand slowly across her forehead. "I just got back from Peru this morning and it was exhausting."

Kate looks at her sharply, but Joey is not being impish; that mood has vanished.

Kate says, "You mean you dreamt you'd been away?"

"No," Joey says. "Not that. It wasn't dreaming. It was travelling."

"But you've never been to Peru."

"Now I have, silly."

"Do you know where you are now?"

"This again. Of course I do. People are always asking where I am. Why do they keep losing track of me? I'm on 12C, room 75, Brigham and Women's—what an absurd name for a hospital, isn't it? A particular and a general." Joey extends her long slim hand and Kate leans toward the bed and puts hers into it. "Now," Joey says, not quite mockingly, "Tell me about your squirrels."

"I make a paste of sunflower seeds and peanut butter," Kate begins earnestly. "I put it in saucers and put the saucers into the Hav-a-Hart trap and I put the trap in the crawl space in the attic. Then I wait until I hear a mad thrashing.

I go up and carry the trap downstairs and let the squirrel out in the garden."

"Does it work?"

"Too well, that's the problem. So far it's eight squirrels, and that may be too many for a family. I'm probably just giving them a free trip downstairs. I'm recycling squirrels."

"I think you must be. You have to drive them across town, you know. But be sure to take them all to the same place. Of course, if you want to prove they're the same ones that you keep taking downstairs, get hair spray." She pauses, then says, "Your twins will know which one. I think it's called 'Streaks and Tips Pink-Glo.' Spray them a bit before you let them loose in the garden. Then if you find a pink squirrel in your attic, you'll know the truth. Besides," she grinned. "It's phosphorescent. You'll be the only one on your block with squirrels who glow in the night."

Outside, dusk has fallen. The street lights have come on. Joey's room has gotten almost dark, except for a shaft of light from the door.

"Tell me something," Kate says slowly. "Have you been other places besides Peru? These days I mean."

"Two days ago I went to Georgia. I drove back all night. Before that, Washington, DC. It always tires me out."

"But you know you're in the hospital now?"

"Of course, silly. What do you think?"

Kate has given up pacing the room; she doesn't feel like racing around any more. Instead, she sits enveloped in stillness in the armchair by the bed, watching Joey's face, pale and moonlike. "Tell me something else," Kate says. "About Mom: you know she can't really be annoyed at you first of all, because you're wonderful, and second of all, because she's been dead for many years, right? So, it was probably—let's say—more of a dream, right?"

"Of course Mom's been dead, they've all been dead for years, Wise One." Joey looks at her knowingly and seriously. "I only said that," she talks more rapidly now. "I only said that because when we came to this hospital and you got out of the ambulance before I did because you wanted to make sure everything was all right, and you were looking all beautiful and wise because you were the birthday girl, not the other one, and you climbed up the tree by the main building and you found out that the squirrels have their own webwork of passages along the limbs of all the trees so they don't ever need to come down to street level, but can get anywhere they need to up there, jumping across the spaces sometimes and swaying, but you didn't have to jump, did you Katie, you just leaned from the star-burst of that leafless oak, and you stretched over to the ivy on the outside of the building and you held onto it for a while, just breathing in and out—in that way you have when you're upset—and then you started climbing again, until you got to that white clump, high in the ivy, and you found out it really was a ghost after all, and you sniffed it a bit and wrinkled the front of your face and poked it to see if it was a bag of loose bones or what, and then you climbed higher to try to get to that little room on the third floor, to ask the man there about all this."

Joey stops and sweeps her free arm as though to indicate

herself, the room, the outside.

Kate goes over to her and places her palm once more on her sister's cheek. Joey, exhausted and silent now, moves Kate's hand up to her forehead, then to the top of her head where the stitches are. She holds Kate's hand there and Kate can feel the bristling ends of the threads and the soft, optimistic stubble of Joey's hair. Joey looks drowsy from the pills and soon it will be time to leave her.

Kate will go home. There, her mysterious daughters and her husband will have cooked dinner. On the dining room table will be a long narrow box delivered that afternoon by Federal Express—a birthday present which Joey has ordered for her, two weeks early. The box contains a thick spray of yellow orchids, the first of a subscription of tropical blooms which will arrive every month for the next year, each bearing a card in Joey's name.

Over the meal, Daniel and the girls will ask Kate about Joey's condition, but she will avoid telling them much until she has thought more about it. She will not uncover the right word for it until she finds herself still awake, listening for squirrels, at the quietest hour.

Life in the Temperate Zone

I T WAS THREE IN THE MORNING. SUSANNA HAD BEEN UP WITH the baby; as she was going back to bed she heard noises in Finsson's yard. From her window she saw someone slip into the Icelander's station wagon and make furtive attempts to start it. The motor turned over, coughed, died. Then whoever it was—she thought it was a man—left the car and rustled around under the porch, emerging with a bicycle. When he mounted the bike and rode it into the street it wobbled uncontrollably; he walked it back and propped it against the car. Susanna wondered whether to yell out the window, or throw something, but she hesitated: so far he hadn't succeeded in stealing anything—he had just made unsuccessful attempts to sample her neighbor's vehicles. But when he started pushing at Finsson's porch door, quietly forcing the latch, she went into her bedroom and called the police. She tried to wake her husband, Robert. He said, "You handle it, honey. You take care of it," and went back to sleep.

The police drove up and were soon questioning the tall

man in the Icelander's living room. He paced back and forth, pointing to various houses on the street, and then took out his wallet and spread his identification cards on the coffee table. Susanna realized that she had called the police on her new neighbor, Leif Finsson, in his own house. As she returned to bed she tried to wake Robert again, to tell him of her embarrassment, but he rolled over, muttering dreamily.

When their two-year-old, Robin, woke them at dawn with her crowing and laughter, Robert, refreshed by his untroubled night, suggested they all take a walk before breakfast. "I want to copulate with that sky," he said, striding down the middle of the street, his arms outstretched. "Don't you feel it, Susu?"

Robert was a painter. In the early days, Susanna had found his outbursts and pronouncements odd and beguiling; no one in her lab spoke like that. At the beginning of their courtship Robert had taken her to visit a taxidermist friend of his, an old Italian in the North End who had been preparing a pheasant for Robert so that it was just the plumage and the skin, hollow. When they left the taxidermist's place, they spent the rest of the night wandering through the sleeping city, Robert with the bird on his head like some strange plumed helmet. As she matched her stride to his, Susanna glanced up at his face from time to time and wondered how she could become a part of his life. They ended up in Cambridge, on the banks of the Charles, at dawn.

∞

Now she looked up at the sunstruck sky, her eyes gritty and prosaic. Robin was clinging around her neck, smelling of milk, damp and warm and curly-headed.

"Don't you feel it?" he said again.

She said nothing. What she wanted most were nights of uninterrupted sleep, days of thinking about insects, then perhaps evenings of love. With a human, not the sky.

"You don't, do you," he answered. "You would rather think about it than dance to it." He dropped his arms. "Analyze it; chop it into diagrams. Go ahead: work out the genetics of human crossed with sky."

She wondered. He seemed so intent on diverging them, defining them apart. She kept silent. The hemlock by Finsson the Icelander's house was thicker than ever, due to the summer rains. Across the street, Pilky Hammond's sycamore—Cambridge ladies had always been fond of sycamores—had fresh scaly patches of olive and yellow. Although the immense magnolia, brought back from China by Ross Hammond's grandfather, had lost its suggestive fruits and now showed clusters of orange seeds, it still smelled of cinnamon. The black oak in front of their own house had just been carved to a strange shape by the telephone company, whose lines ran between its branches. Loose flocks of blue jays were coming in each day from the north as the local jays moved on.

But though the smells were not yet those of autumn—there wasn't any wood smoke yet, none of the deep tannins of rain-brewed leaves—the September sky seemed both intimate and distant and she knew she should catch and hold onto its pulsing golden light.

∞

Mailys arrived later that day. Susanna opened the door and the tall black girl's beauty hit her in the face, in the stomach, in the heart. Susanna almost didn't let her in. This wasn't what I meant when I said we'd take a boarder, she thought. I had in mind a faceless paying guest, not some thorn, some reminder of everything I am not.

Susanna took hold of her panic and shook it. Come off it, she told herself, it's just beauty. She inhaled deeply, wondering if she should get some sun on her own pale skin, if she should grow her bushy black hair until it was that long. "Well," she said, finally. "Why don't you come in?" She tried to smile at this young woman who was to live with them during her last year in high school, Mailys Livingston from Jamaica. Her parents were off somewhere, diplomatically. Mailys meaning 'May-Lily.' Mother from Guadeloupe, father Jamaican, such a dark flaming lily, their girl. She wouldn't be any help in the house, beauty gets in the way of helpfulness. Susanna was glad Robert was out; perhaps the girl's radiance would fade before he came back. If not, could he stand it? Could the neighborhood stand it?

In the afternoon, Susanna was working in the garden. With the edge of her trowel she hacked at a maple root which was preventing her from digging where she wanted. The smell of earthmold and the warmth of the sun on her neck made her smile. A shadow fell in front of her. Finsson is leaning over my fence, she thought. I'm going to have to apologize.

"So you called the police on me last night, your own

neighbor." His voice was low and full of self-mocking mournfulness, the music of his Icelandic accent sounding ancient and bardic.

"Oh, God. I'm so sorry," said Susanna. She stood up suddenly, shading her eyes from the sun and pointed toward his car with her trowel. "I thought someone was trying to steal your car, and your bike—or break into your house. I thought you were away. I didn't know what to do."

Finsson explained that he had been in Iceland, his flight was delayed and he had caught the last connecting plane to Boston. When he got in, he went to visit friends and stayed very late. When he finally got home, he found that he had car keys but no house keys, and so decided to spend the night with a lady friend. But the car kept stalling and he didn't want to wake his neighbors. Then his bicycle tires were flat. "So finally I broke into my own house," he lamented, still smiling. "I didn't know you were watching."

"I hope you're not upset."

"No, no. I just had a hard time convincing the police that this is my house." His license still had his old address, his passport said Reykjavik; his business in Cambridge was unclear.

A week later Mailys was sitting on the front steps, doing her homework in the sun, when Finsson's dog, Thorgrimmer, appeared in front of her. The dog was white and gray and brown, shaggy with long bangs over his eyes. "Why do you look at me, dog?" said Mailys.

Thorgrimmer barked.

Finsson had followed and now stood behind his dog. "Perhaps you will come to a movie with me, sometime."

"Out of the question," Mailys said. "How old are you anyway?"

Finsson, who was thirty-five, did a rapid estimation of her upper limit for a date. "How does twenty-seven sound?" he asked.

She shook her head.

"I don't mean a date, then," he said. "What about tea?"

"Tea?"

Finsson smiled. "You're right," he said, teasingly. "I shouldn't be bothering you. You have your homework, my little *au pair* girl."

"I am not an '*au pair*'," Mailys corrected him. "I am a paying guest. I am not their servant and I am not *your* little anything. OK?"

"But we are neighbors, after all," Finsson said. "And neighbors have tea. Besides, we have something in common, you and I: we're islanders."

She looked at his craggy pale face, his blond fleece, and wondered out loud, "What is that supposed to mean?"

"Oh, no," he teased. "You have homework. I will tell you about it later."

She bent her head over her book.

Pilky Hammond, a plaid kitchen apron over her blue denim skirt, was mowing her lawn. She kept an eye on the interview between the Icelander and the Jamaican girl, and when Finsson turned to leave, she crossed the street to intercept him.

"I wanted to come and greet you when you first moved in last month, but I was afraid you'd think I was just a dotty old lady." She held out her hand. "Pilky Hammond," she said. "Short for Priscilla or maybe Pulchritude—it's been so long, I forget which."

"Leif Finsson," he said. "Short for nothing."

Pilky Hammond looked him up and down. She smiled and said, "I see." Then she said in a smoke-burnished growl, "Listen, what about a drink? I have some really super gin. Come on, I'll just tether my lawn mower out back."

Finsson studied her carefully as though Cambridge ladies in academic neighborhoods were wondrous animals. Like Pilky here, mowing all morning with a push-mower, *click, click, clickety*, with that cigarette stuck to her bottom lip. Finsson had already met Pilky's husband, Ross, who planted gnarled and twisted little bushes on his lawn. Meant to look Chinese, he said. Although a pure New Englander, Ross was apparently some kind of Chinese scholar—directed one of the libraries at the University. "Yes," Finsson said to Pilky Hammond. "I will drink with you."

Together they crossed the street with the dog Thorgrimmer trotting along behind. There, in Pilky's kitchen, they stayed with each other, drinking and talking the afternoon away.

When Finsson left Pilky's house, the sky had turned a deep sudden blue and the just-lit lamps cast an orange glow. It was that time of day which draws the sharpest distinction between those who are already home and those who must still walk through the twilight with the night hard on their heels.

On the last day of September, a Friday, the air paused, aching and sultry, waiting for the hurricane. Narrow clouds slid into a hazy blue sky; more invaded, padding the blue with layers, thick and cottony at first, then bruised and purplish around the edges. The wind nibbled at the outskirts of the Chinese magnolia; the maple leaves gave a tentative shimmy. The radio weatherman said, "Well, Boston, batten down the hatches: we're looking down the gun-barrel."

Susanna and Mailys were sticking long X's of masking tape on the windows. Susanna was whistling to herself. It was only when she stopped to climb down from the dining room table that she heard Mailys singing softly in the front hall, as though in response.

Robert carried Robin into the kitchen to play. "Don't forget the candles," he called to Susanna. "Let's have them everywhere. I bought cartons of them. I got charcoal, we can grill things in the fireplace. We can have a feast. I got a bag of apples; should I make a pie or something? Will you tell me how? Do we have time?"

Mailys touched Susanna's arm. "Let us go outside." They stepped onto the porch to feel the beginning pulses of the wind.

Pilky Hammond, who was cutting her chrysanthemums, darted across the street to them. "It's going to be quite wonderful," she said, looking around. "Here, take some of these flowers. Ross and I can't eat them all." Laughing, she thrust the yellow and russet flowers into Susanna's arms then took a pack of cigarettes from her apron pocket and lit one. The smoke from her cigarette trailed north and then south, as though the wind were undecided.

"Leif called a few minutes ago from New York," Pilky said. She paused as if conjuring up an image of Finsson's existence there. "He asked if I could tape his windows as the storm may get here before he does. He's driving. But here's the thing." She took a long drag from her cigarette and exhaled slowly. "I haven't even done my place yet, and I've misplaced Ross—he wandered out a while ago to hunt for flashlight batteries." She looked over her shoulder as though Ross might have suddenly turned up. "Do you think you could start on Leif's windows, if I give you his key?"

Susanna nodded.

"Oh," Pilky remembered. "Don't worry about Thorgrimmer—I've got him at my house." She waved her cigarette, as though to say, When you're as old as I am, you become the protector of everyone in the place.

As she taped up the Icelander's windows, Susanna found herself looking into her own house. Robert danced around Robin in her playpen, then turned to sketch on a tall narrow canvas. These days he was working on a series of vertical boundaries: cracks of windows; edges of tree-trunks against sky; a tall thin woman in a narrow doorway. She had asked him who the woman was, but he answered only that it was one of his models. Susanna knew he tended to sleep with most of the women he painted, he had warned her about that from the beginning. He had said it was his way of doing things, that he needed such affairs as a pressure valve. It will keep me sweeter to you, he explained. Periodically he would leave for several days, and return with a new set of portraits. But in between he charmed her with his sweetness. This is how I am, he told her; I don't like it but I don't know how to change it. She had thought she could show him how to change. When that failed, she would learn to live with it. In the end, it turned out not to be a problem.

Susanna watched as Mailys came to the door of Robert's studio and spoke to him, keeping her hand on the door frame. Susanna wondered at the mood between them, whether Robert had begun to court Mailys yet. He was talking now, pointing to the girl and to his canvas. He walked over to her, put his hand on her chin and turned her face toward the light. Then he stepped back as though dancing and said something, raising his arms. Mailys raised her arms; then she laughed and shook her head, breaking her pose. The baby stood in her playpen and whirled her arms in circles, laughing. Mailys was smiling at both of them as she left the room. Soon Susanna could see her going from room to room with candles.

Across the street, white stripes were appearing on the Hammond's windows, with Pilky gesticulating energetically behind them. Susanna had the feeling that Pilky had been bestowing something in giving her the keys to Finsson's house. Here, in the fireplace, the logs were set; on the floor, shaggy white sheepskins formed a sort of nest.

When she finished with the living room, Susanna taped the kitchen windows. She opened the refrigerator: four bottles of Akvavit in the freezer compartment, one of them half empty. A jar of herring, half a round of pumpernickel. Butter. No fruit, no vegetables. She would invite him for a meal.

Upstairs there were no large windows to tape but she wanted to look anyway. The Icelander's bed was wide and low, covered with a striped blanket of gray and white and brown wool. It was an immense bed; the wooden frame looked hand hewn. Without thinking, she pulled back the covers. She wanted to see Finsson's sheets. There: brick red. She felt them: pure cotton. She wasn't sure what they told her. Not enough. Sitting down on the red cotton she opened the drawer of the bedside table: condoms, an Icelandic *New Testament*, a flashlight, a box of dark chocolate mints of a brand she didn't know. She took a chocolate, unwrapped it, and popped it in her mouth. He's my neighbor, she thought, and I'm responsible for him: I have to know what chocolate he eats. She took another.

A flash of lightning outside the window and a low rumble of thunder brought Susanna to her feet. Outside, the sky was darkening to greenish purple. She closed the drawer and straightened the bed covers. She hurried through his bureau drawers, looking for something different. That's what she was looking for: differences. She didn't want Finsson to be the same as Robert. She didn't want men to be all the same. Her fingers touched a box in the back of a drawer, behind crumpled underwear. She pulled it out, setting it on the top of the bureau. The box was heavy and made of a variegated wood she didn't recognize. Inside, nested in coils of white sheepswool, were shells in the form of small volcanoes: barnacles. They were cast in massive silver. As she pondered their steady, anchoring, weight in her palm, a ripping crack of thunder startled her out of her explorations.

The storm hit with full force in mid-afternoon. The wind roared up the street, bending the elm, oaks, and maples. It swirled the curved boughs of the Chinese magnolia and gave the hemlock a mad waltz.

Robert carried chairs out to the front porch, which was protected from the wind by the angle of the house. He had made a large bowl of popcorn. "Come, Susu, come out for a bit," he called to her. When she didn't respond, he went back into the house and called again, "Hey, you're not going to stay inside, are you? When we have a storm like this? Don't burrow-in today—your crawly things can wait." He paused, got no answer, and said, "Mailys thinks you should come out and watch. Don't you, Mailys?"

At her desk, Susanna closed her book reluctantly. For the past few months, Robert had been calling her insects "crawly things." When they had first started living together, three years ago, he had seemed proud of her work. He had asked her to bring home some moths from the lab so he could paint portraits of them. The canvasses had been dazzling and slightly uncanny. But last week he had introduced

her to a friend of his, saying, "This is my wife, she does worms."
He knew that her moths—silkworms—were quite different
from "worms." She understood that it was his way of demoting her on the great chain of being. She got up slowly. He
was already usurping the hurricane. She didn't want to play
his storm games anymore.

When Susanna joined them on the porch Robert jumped
up excitedly. "Do you feel it?" he asked.

What Susanna felt was edgy and breathless, as if the passing gusts were sucking the air from her lungs. Mailys looked
at Susanna's face, and as though guessing her mood handed
her the bowl of popcorn, saying, "Here, have some."

Across the street, Pilky Hammond waved to them from
her front window, and Ross, behind her, gestured vaguely.
Finsson hadn't come home yet. The rain sheeted to a river
on the asphalt—so thick that drops seemed to dance upwards
from the water's surface.

Half an hour later when the rain slowed and the wind died
down Pilky and Ross ventured across the street in matching
yellow raincoats and green rubber boots. The air smelt of
split tropical wood and warm islands. Robert carried two more
chairs onto the porch, and refilled the bowl of popcorn. "What
will you drink?" he asked. "Beer? Gin?"

"The clear stuff," Pilky Hammond answered. Ross nodded his concurrence. "Purer, better for you," she added. She
looked for a moment at Mailys, who was sitting on the porch
floor with her arms around her knees.

Mailys smiled dreamily, engulfed by homesickness. She told them that on the wind she could smell the perfume tree, always the first wood to break in storms at home. Underneath, she could smell frangipani flowers. She couldn't stop inhaling until finally she grew dizzy. "Listen," she said. "Sweetsop and soursop and mammee apple. How can those words make me long so for home, when I also want to live here with you forever?" She put her head down, circled in her arms.

No one spoke. Susanna put her hand on the girl's shoulder and kept it there.

The sky glowered yellow, lurking. The wind was quiet.

"It's just the 'eye', isn't it?" Pilky Hammond asked softly.

"Oh yes, there'll be more," Robert said to her. "Worse probably." He smiled. "I'd like to go wading; it's not often you can swim in your own street. It would be a way of possessing it. We could take off our clothes." He gave her a conspiratorial leer. Pilky blushed. She purred and sipped her gin.

Susanna went inside to check on Robin and found her asleep, her rump high in the air and her fist in her mouth. Standing for a moment in the doorway, watching her child sleep through the storm, she felt waves of sadness underneath her vast love. When she looked at Robin everything seemed simple, life reduced to its elements.

Finsson drove up and parked his heaving station wagon in his driveway. Steam leaked from under the hood.

"Come join us," Robert called. Pilky Hammond held up her glass proudly, as though Finsson were her protégé. Mailys glanced at the Icelander with a skeptical smile, her fingers coiling in her black hair. She had finally gone for tea with him a few days earlier.

"Are we really having 'tea'?" she had asked when he opened his door.

"I invited you for 'tea.' This time, that is what we will have. There will be other times."

Sitting on the living room couch with mugs of Oolong, Mailys had tried to tell Finsson about her schoolwork. She began with photosynthesis, but she got tangled in the pathways of captured light. The transformations of energy remained mysterious. Finsson's hand kept finding its way onto her shoulder.

"Listen," she said, turning to look at his hand.

He said, "You know, girl, in Iceland, it is customary to test a maiden's fertility before asking her to marry you."

She replied that where she came from things were done in the opposite order. Anyway, she was not interested in marriage yet. "Is that why you have so many girlfriends?" she asked. "They aren't fertile enough?"

"Oh, no," he laughed. "I like women."

"But you don't love them?"

"I do love them," he protested. "Anyway, I'm not propositioning you. And since I'm not, you shouldn't be minding my hand on your shoulder. It's such a small form of contact." He lifted his hand from her shoulder and put it back lightly, as though to show her how inconsequential it was.

⃝

The wind revived itself, moaning and whistling up the hill. The rain slapped down in sheets. Robert refilled the drinks. Susanna brought out a bowl of carrots and cherry tomatoes; she offered it first to Finsson. As a centipede emerged from between the floorboards of the porch, Robert said, "Oh, look, Susanna. One of your creeping friends."

"Not one of mine," she answered, giving a quizzical look. "Everything that crawls isn't mine."

Robert shrugged. He turned to Finsson, asking, "What were you up to in New York?"

Pilky darted in before Finsson could answer. "He's got this absolutely nifty scheme. He's bringing Iceland to the rest of the world—he will seduce us all by means of haddock." She explained that in Iceland the fishing boats come back to port every couple of days. "Our Finsson can have the fish flown from Reykjavik to New York," she waved her cigarette up the street, as though New York were just out of view. "Then he drives it here, to us, and it will still be much fresher than anything you can buy at the Boston fish pier, because our local boats go out for weeks, you know, and freeze the fish."

"It's all in the back of my car," Finsson broke in. "Two hundred pounds. I'll show you as soon as the rain lets up. Fresh haddock smells like roses."

A squall of wind slapped against the trees. Thunder growled. Finsson was quiet for a bit, then said, "You know, when I was about the age of Mailys here—Iceland had the bad luck to declare Prohibition." He said this a melancholy voice. "For a country so far north, that can have tragic consequences."

As he talked, he drew out his A's and O's until they were long and dark. Mailys was smiling. Finsson watched her face. He looked at her wild hair and her blackness as though he wanted to take her to his house and sit beside her and run his fingers up and down the skin of her bare arms, as though he wondered what her body would look like stretched out next to his. "Well," he said, tipping back in his chair and finding the way into his story. "We took the steamer to Norway, my friend and I, to the port town of Bergen. There we chartered a fishing boat, to carry us back to a fjord near Reykjavik... us and our dear cargo."

"Which was?" asked Mailys.

"Akvavit, my girl." He smiled. "Water of life. Made from potatoes and tasting like caraway seeds."

Mailys looked dubious.

"We spent every penny we had, to rent the boat and buy the liquor. We were going to make a hoard of money. Icelanders were desperate: they were distilling anything they could liquefy, and making themselves sick." Finsson stood up and leaned against the porch railing.

Mailys watched his face.

"Two days and two nights it took us from Bergen by boat." Finsson looked at Mailys. "Do you know the northern lights?" She shook her head.

"Any of you?" He looked around at the others. None of them had seen the northern lights except Pilky Hammond who nodded vigorously, puffing on her cigarette.

"They take up the sky: curtains of greenish white, weaving and dancing, ribbons streaked with purple and red. It feels as though they're trying to tell you things and you're just on the edge of understanding. Sometimes you're even sure you can hear them, like the flapping of a sail or the swishing of cloth. Under their spell you stay up all night.

"The danger is that you forget to watch for icebergs." He looked out at the blowing trees for a moment, then went on. "Our course lay just at the southern limit of drift ice. At the end of summer, large chunks break off the mother floes and travel on their own." He leaned on the back of his chair. "Have you seen icebergs, then?"

Mailys, who had been sinking into his story, shook her head slowly. The wind dropped, leaving only the clapping sound of the rain. Finsson continued, more softly:

"You have to see them up close, icebergs, with the sun behind them. At heart they are blue-green, you want to go deep into them. They don't seem cold. Weird, they look, and… welcoming.

"By the second night we were just off the coast of Iceland, right where the Gulf Stream hits the East Greenland Current. It was September; a warm breeze was blowing from the tropics, from your Caribbean." He pointed accusingly at Mailys. She sat up, ready to defend her climate, her self.

Finsson said, in a lower voice, "We lost everything. We had been looking at the sky all night and we didn't see the iceberg until we were on top of it."

"Oh, gosh," said Pilky Hammond. "Weren't you absolutely terrified?"

"Didn't you freeze?" asked Susanna.

"Both. When we slammed into the ice and it crunched the boat apart, the lurching and that sound of wood ripping, it just knocks the soul out of you. We kept afloat by holding onto chunks of wreckage. The Coast Guard out of Reykjavik picked us up, my friend, our Norwegian captain, and me." Finsson nodded at Susanna. "We were completely frozen." He crossed his arms, and placed his hands under his armpits as though they still needed warming. Mailys crossed her arms.

"They suspected that we were smuggling Akvavit but the crates had sunk, so they had no proof. And so…" He paused, saw that Mailys was totally engaged with his telling, and went on. "It seemed better to leave the country for a while. That was when I made my first trip to the States."

The wind came to life again, roaring up the street with a thousand howls. While it had seemed before like some over-sized but domesticated animal, now its full wildness showed. The sky shimmered and scolded. On the porch, the neigh-bors pulled their chairs back towards the house but a sudden shift in wind direction drove the sheeting rain onto them. Robert, carrying his chair, led the way, saying, "Come on in. Let's get dry and we can make something to eat." They settled, heaving and laughing, around the kitchen table.

After she had put her chair inside, Susanna came out alone to the porch and walked out into the street inhaling the storm and letting the rain soak her. It plastered her shirt and jeans to her body, it drenched her hair and streamed down her face. Her sneakers filled with water. In the force of the wind, the trees on both sides of the street heaved toward her and away, as though focusing their dance on her. She spun around to see if they were all bending toward her at the same moment, and wondering what the shape of the wind must be to make them do that. But when the sky went white with lightning followed with immediate growls of thunder, she ran up the front steps, grabbed the popcorn bowl and went inside.

Thus no one was watching Pilky Hammond's sycamore as it battled the wind: the largest branch split off and skittered down the street out of control; and no one saw the newly trimmed black oak in front of Susanna and Robert's porch as it tangled with the telephone wires, pulling them loose with a small blue flash which sizzled along the line.

Late the next afternoon, Pilky Hammond was gathering the dead branches from her lawn and stacking them by the side of her house. She walked slowly, with a slight limp. Finsson, crossing the street, noticed the sag of her body, the unkempt look of her hair. He bent down and put his arm around her shoulders. "Well, Pilky my dear—how would you and Ross like fish for dinner? I have heaps of fresh haddock for you." He told her he had been unable to sell his fish because they hadn't been scaled. Two hundred pounds of haddock lay in makeshift ice chests in his kitchen.

After packing Pilky's freezer with fish, then Susanna's, Finsson spent the rest of the afternoon pushing a market carriage through the Cambridge neighborhood, a shaggy Thorgrimmer expectantly trotting by his side. A sign on the carriage read, "FRESH FISH, DIRECT FROM ICELAND." Balanced on top of the fish crate was Susanna's baby scale.

On Sunday morning Susanna was vacuuming the upstairs hall. From the window she could look down into Finsson's house. His curtains, where there were any, came only halfway up. She was waiting for Finsson and his new red-headed girl-friend to appear in his living room. Some days they would chase each other through the house with no clothes on. Then they would disappear upstairs. Once she had seen them running from opposite directions into the living room where they collapsed in laughter on the sheepskin rugs by the fire-place. Thorgrimmer pranced around them, barking. Finsson got up and shooed him into the kitchen, closing the door. From behind her curtains, Susanna had watched as they made love on the sheepskins.

Today Finsson and his lady friend brought their breakfast on trays to the rugs—tall glasses of orange juice, and plates of toast. They pulled all the cushions down from the couch. The Sunday papers were spread out beside them.

The next afternoon Susanna came home from the lab to find Robin kicking and crying in her high chair. Boxes of cereal littered the floor.

"Bugs," Robert shouted. "There were worms in the cereal I tried to give Robin. Everything is crawling."

"Really?" Susanna spoke softly, in a manner that she knew infuriated Robert because of its calmness. "Wait," she said smoothly. "Let me take a look."

Robert was not in the mood to wait. "Science? Is this what science is, growing your stinking animals in the cereal?" He grabbed a box from the cupboard, opened the flap, shaking the rice out onto the counter. "There," he said. "Look at them. Why can't you keep your maggots in your fucking lab? All the boxes have these strings, worms, moths, everywhere." He ripped open packages of Saltines and Triscuits and graham crackers and emptied them. "Even King-fucking-Arthur." He showered the bag of flour onto the floor.

The front door opened and Mailys came in from school. She took off her backpack in the dining room, looked at Susanna and Robert and the mess in the kitchen and said, "Why don't I take Robin for a walk?" Susanna gave a grateful shrug. Robin, in her high chair, stopped whimpering and lifted her arms to be carried away.

Susanna's neck was tingling; Robert's anger had finally ignited her own. "It's just Ephestia, you ass," she said. "*Ephestia kuhniella*, the 'meal moth'. A lepidopteran." She walked to the sink, turning her back to him so the redness of her cheeks wouldn't show him he had gotten to her.

"Just Ephestia, Rob," he mimicked her. "Christ," he said, addressing the kitchen cabinets. "She even knows the Latin name for fucking maggots."

"Well, somebody's got to know something," she said. He was such a stupid bastard she couldn't think why she lived with him. "We can't all spend our days smearing pigment and looking for moonbeams to dance in."

"No, I guess scientists wouldn't do anything as messy as painting or dancing, would they. They just feed their babies with neat little chunky crispy maggots. When they can bother to come home and feed them at all."

Robert leaned over the counter and began patting the spilled rice into a thin layer, then tracing designs in it with his fingers. At the other side of the room, Susanna turned the water on full and started to wash the day's accumulation of pots and dishes. They were pleasingly loud as she let them bang and clank together.

After a while her anger gave way to sadness. "Hey, don't be this way," she said finally. "What's eating you?"

"Worms," he said, more calmly. "They're eating everything."

"But Rob, they're really not so bad." She turned off the water and crossed the room. "Look, these are the cocoons." She scraped a grayish patch the size of a rice grain from the back wall of the cupboard. She showed it to him on her finger. He looked at it without interest, then took a spatula from the counter and hunkered down among the boxes on the floor. She went on, "The strings are just their silk. They hatch into little salt and pepper-colored moths. They come in the grains we buy. From the store. I didn't bring them home. There aren't any at the lab. Nobody I know is working on them—besides, they're not harmful, I mean they don't *do* anything to you."

"They disgust me." He poked with his spatula at a pile of Rice Krispies. "You wouldn't be so scientifically objective," he said coldly, "if you had seen your child's cereal crawling."

"Look, I'll show you how to get rid of them. It will take us ten minutes."

Susanna crossed over to Robert, stepping between the

boxes and around the whale-shaped mound of flour. She wiped her hands on her jeans then put them on his shoulders. When he didn't reject her touch, she sat down on the floor behind him and began to rub his neck. She saw that she could only bring peace this way for a limited time. Their cycles of exhilaration and exhaustion were getting more frequent and more vicious; the let-down after the fierceness was cold and harrowing. She worked her hands up his spine, knuckling it softly. She could feel him relaxing, but she felt so distant from him that she was glad not to have to see his face. Though they would make love in a few minutes, on her part it would be a mercy fuck, full of pity and sadness.

Finsson sat at Pilky Hammond's kitchen table, his head in his hands. In the middle of the table stood a bottle of Icelandic Akvavit, half gone. Finsson's fish business had run into new problems: although this week's batch of four hundred pounds had arrived from Iceland already scaled, a pair of Italian businessmen had warned him away from the Boston fish pier, saying fish in Boston was their territory. He would have to peddle from his market carriage again. "It was really such a good idea," he said.

Pilky Hammond poured them each more Akvavit, inhaled deeply on her cigarette. She sighed happily, as though she liked having this Icelander in her Cambridge house, bringing her his troubles and his bottle of clear liquor; as though his lanky presence and his knees just fitting under her table made her kitchen complete. She considered his business, asked him if he had a pen, and neatly ripping open a used envelope to expose the clean rectangle of its unused side, she wrote down a list of local private schools and hospitals which might want to buy his fish. Watching her, Finsson felt secure and cared for. "Pilky," he said. "You are an angel."

"Oh, no," she said, in a rush of self-exposure. "I am the street witch. I go down the street and pull everyone's trash cans back from the sidewalks after the truck passes. I rip off the notices people tack to telephone poles, to eliminate clutter. I complain to the papers about night sky pollution. I am getting older. I care about my garden, my wounded sycamore and Ross's Chinese trees. And Ross, of course."

Mailys asked Susanna what she should do about Robert's request to sit for a portrait.

"Tell me first what you think," said Susanna.

"He seems so sad these days." Mailys began to pace. "I don't know if it would cheer him, though he says it would."

"Do you have enough time?" asked Susanna. "How is school going?"

"He said I could be reading. That's not the problem, the problem is…" She stopped pacing, sat down against the wall.

"Ah," said Susanna. "He wants your clothes off. Is that it?"

"Mmn… I guess so."

Tell him to go bugger himself, Susanna thought. The bastard. "It's completely up to you, you know, what you want to wear, if you decide to sit for him. He does lots of people fully clothed, so don't let him bully you. He's also done lots of nudes.

You'll find it intense to be looked at so much, and flattering, at first. But you've got to remember, he's not a doctor."

"What does that mean?"

"There won't be any pretense that he's not human and you're not human. It's all personal—when he chooses. It also flickers back and forth: you'll think he's seeing you as you, and you'll realize that he finds you beautiful and suddenly you'll be an object on which the light is falling. You'll disintegrate into questions of shadows, planes and volumes. Then he'll start to leer at you again. He uses all of it. Anyway, you think about it and decide."

"Listen, can I ask you something else?"

"Go ahead."

"Why does he keep accusing you?"

"Of what?"

"Of, well, about not having sharp enough senses."

"Oh, that." She was about to give a small dismissive laugh but she stifled it. She wasn't ready for this question. She had been avoiding it for months.

"I mean, he's completely wrong, so why does he say it?"

Susanna looked at Mailys. She studied her seventeen year-old bluntness. "I don't know," she said. "We are grating on each other. Look, when I first knew him I wanted to graft myself onto his limbs. I wanted to see everything through his eyes. I wanted all his insights, his instincts. I was greedy to be one with him. I thought about giving up biology in order to study painting. I had confused submergence with being in love. He really liked me that way."

"What changed you?"

"I don't know. Maybe it was being pregnant with Robin.

Suddenly the practical world had to be faced and conquered. This small divergence turned into a wedge. He sees it as 'reason' as opposed to 'feeling.' He has always felt that if he even looked at it—at the maintenance of the practical world—it would suck him dry, ruin his ability to work. When I ask him things like 'Shouldn't we get the car inspected?' or 'What shall we have for dinner?'—these are not innocent propositions, to him. They make him feel hunted, in danger of being smothered by daily life. He says they are like the old snare for pheasants: fresh green peas strung on a black thread. The unsuspecting bird pecks and eats until the thread tangles in his gullet and he chokes to death." She paused. "Does this make any sense to you?"

Mailys nodded.

Susanna said, "Nothing about love is simple."

Finsson watched from his living room window as Mailys took her shirt off in Robert's studio. He could see Robert trace the air around the blackness of her nipples with his finger tips.

Finsson stood there, his hands on the window frame; he said something in Icelandic. Then Mailys reached behind her for her shirt. She put it back on. She settled in the yellow canvas butterfly chair, a thick book on her lap. Robert turned back to his tubes of paint and his palette. Finsson said, in English: Tea. Oh God, it's time for that girl to come over again for tea.

"Do you want to try some food from my country?" Finsson asked Mailys the next afternoon. She nodded. He brought out pickled herring and black bread, a bottle of Akvavit.

"Corruption of minors," she said, smiling.

"Education," Finsson said. "This is my national dish." He paused. "I mainly eat it when I am here. When I am in Reykjavik, I eat 'American style.' I grill steaks outside, even in winter. I bring American beefsteaks back with me when I go." He spread some herring on a slice of black bread and carried it to Mailys. "Once you live in a new place too long… you get homesick for that place, too, when you leave it." He crossed the room and sat, not very close to her, on the sofa. He stretched out his arm placing his hand on her shoulder, lightly so as not to startle her. Mailys sat still, accepting his hand there, wanting it.

"Nostalgia has as many loves as I do." He raised his fingers and let them tangle themselves in her black hair, playing slowly, and, as if what he was doing didn't matter, he talked on, soothing her and warning her—although it was too late—about places and seasons, about homesickness and lovesickness. "Be careful, girl," he said. "You'll miss the ringing gold of autumn here, and the skulking bitch-whip of winter. You'll look for blue-jays on your tropical island, and when you don't find them it will seem the less for it. You'll find you have to leave your island and come back here."

By the end of the autumn, Finsson was selling Icelandic haddock to several schools and hospitals. Mailys had invited him to visit her in Jamaica over Christmas, and he was going to combine seeing her with leading a tour group of thirty Icelandic teenagers to Jamaica for the holidays.

Susanna drove them both to the airport, talking nervously the whole time. She felt she had not taken advantage of Finsson's existence. Mailys had done that, she thought; Mailys had appreciated him. Susanna was envious. She could imagine them in Jamaica—Finsson and his Icelandic teenagers staying in slightly seedy bungalows. By day they would give their pale bodies to the sea; after sunset they would gorge themselves on rum and ganja. Then Finsson would visit Mailys, who would be staying with her parents. With her windows wide open they would lie in bed and listen to the songs of tree frogs and the night breezes rustling through the banana palms. They would make love and fall asleep in each other's arms. Leaving in the early morning Finsson would fold his long legs and climb out the window so as not to wake the household. Finsson was too old for Mailys, Susanna thought.

At home, in the Cambridge winter, Susanna and Robert found themselves heaving and jousting through the final days of their marriage. Their fights had grown louder, with Mailys gone, and their daily language more bitter. Fatigue set in more quickly after the excitement; periods of intense quiet followed each fight. It was no longer possible to separate the strands of their various disagreements, everything was so linked, twisted, knotted. Susanna found that her body was in revulsion toward his. This surprised her as though her body had an independent mind. It was not a sexual coldness, but a fierce heat against his touch, an anger ignited in her whenever their bodies got too close. She hid its nature, however, and he mistook its source for an older form of passion.

Then came the news of Finsson's death. Susanna and Robert began by arguing about grief, and finished by agreeing that their marriage was over.

New Year's Eve. In her kitchen, Susanna was offering drinks to Pilky Hammond. Ross would be over shortly. Robert was upstairs putting Robin to bed. Mailys, who had come back from Jamaica that afternoon, looking leaden and blotchy, was dressing for dinner.

Susanna placed a bottle of Akvavit, unopened, among the other bottles on the counter.

Pilky Hammond said, "Ah." She tapped a cigarette on the table and lit it.

"He gave it to us before he went to Jamaica," Susanna said. "As a present." She paused to catch her breath. "He said to save some for him and we would drink it together when he got back."

"Well," said Pilky. "I think we have to drink it in his honor."

Susanna nodded. She knew she had to say more, and that Pilky Hammond was the only person she could say it to. She remembered the way Pilky had given her the keys to Finsson's house on the day of the hurricane. "I feel so dumb," she blurted. "I let him slip. I didn't focus on him enough, I barely knew him. And now..." she stopped speaking and began to rearrange the bottles on the counter.

"I know," said Pilky Hammond. "If you don't grab hold, people can simply pass through and disappear."

Ross rang at the front door and Susanna ran to let him in. He embraced her warmly, thanked her for inviting them, and uttered something about the new year, smiling and motioning with one of his hands as though he couldn't quite find the proper words.

Mailys, dressed in purple wool, came in and greeted them. Her hair was coiled on top of her head. She looked older; she carried herself with a slow grace born of new doubts. Sitting down next to Susanna she laid her head briefly on Susanna's shoulder in a wordless embrace.

Robert joined them. He kissed Pilky Hammond and shook hands with Ross.

"Look," Pilky Hammond said to Mailys, abruptly, before the usual chatter could start. "I hate to ask you this, but would you mind terribly telling us about it?"

Mailys told what she knew. It had been ten days since Finsson's death. She was still wrapped up in it. Although she hadn't been with him when it happened, it had become her story to tell. She was its guardian.

She told how each night Finsson would take his rented van and drive to all the local bars, bringing back his teenagers and sometimes carrying them from the van to their beds. One night after he had gathered most of his charges, the van had broken down. He borrowed a motorcycle from a barkeeper to search for the few who were still missing.

It was that night in winter when the crabs come up from the sea to spawn, their dark humped shapes gliding jerkily across the moonlit road. Above the roar of the surf, the moon cast smears of silver on the sea, and long shadows across the asphalt shone almost white in the moonlight. She told how he would have ridden his motorcycle at first so slowly through the rounded forms that the motor coughed, stalled, coasted, dead quiet, caught, roared again, and Finsson, leaning back, then forward, laughing into the wind, edging smoothly around a moon-shadowed crab—helmets, he would have thought, the road is crowded with helmets, black breasts, sea creatures crossing over the land tonight—he would have been revving the engine and laughing deep, inhaling the sea air, as he wove through the darkened moving forms in a slow lurching slalom to his death.

"Damnedest thing," Ross said, shaking his head, when she had finished. As though for him it was just another of the many inexplicable aspects of life.

"A season," said Pilky Hammond. "He really only stayed here with us for the autumn."

Susanna wanted causality, explanations. "Had he been drinking?"

"I think it just… happened," Mailys said. "When the crabs come, it's too dangerous. No one drives on the coast road. It's only one or two nights a year."

As they all backstitched again through the story Susanna got up to look at the roast in the oven. She was glad to have everyone here with her for New Year's Eve. She needed people around her at the moment. Even Robert. He seemed calm and charming now. Tomorrow he would move his clothes and painting equipment to an apartment. The sureness and finality of this decision comforted them both, and they could afford a sweetness to each other that had long been absent.

∞

It was 2 A.M. on New Year's Day; Susanna sat in her study. She and Robert had made slow, hesitant, sad love. Unable to sleep afterward, she had left the bedroom so as not to wake him, going first to the kitchen to get some chocolate. Her books lay open on the desk in front of her, but she was nibbling at the bitter chocolate and gazing out the window instead of reading. The street below her window was chafed and white with salt. It was too cold for snow. The windows of Finsson's house were dark. How easy his warmth had seemed, his passions. She wondered if she would ever be capable of such things.

The marriage was over. Her spine tingled at the thought of ending the present chaos. She would plunge herself into the order of work, surrounding herself with insects. Then she would examine the senses. Robert had shaken her confidence in her perceptions by his constant gnawing. "Susanna, you exhibit total sensory numbness," was the way he was fond of putting it. "Only towards you," was her reply. But it is hard not to believe something which is constantly repeated—in marital brainwashing the accusation becomes part of who you are. The marriage had left her streaked with doubt. What if it were more widespread than simple coldness toward him? What if she really were as color-blind, tone-deaf, and so on, down into the soul, as Robert claimed she was? She would figure it out. It was possible—right now her hands and feet did feel numb, with the chill of a sleepless night. Susanna hugged herself for warmth and placed her feet in their red wool socks on the radiator, slipping her toes in between its vertical ribs to gather the heat.

Silk

SUSANNA EDGED OUT OF THE BOUTIQUE INTO THE SHADOWLESS
noon light of Harvard Square. Under her purple tank
top, grey sweatshirt and jeans, she wore the sheath of dusty
rose silk and lace. It was a chilly Friday in April. The impulse
that had led her to steal the silk nightgown was opaque and
inaccessible.

"Well, Robert. What do you think of that?" she asked
aloud. She blushed at the double misbehavior of shoplifting
and talking to herself. She wondered, silently this time, if she
was coming apart.

When she met her friend and lab-mate, Miriam, in the
Indian restaurant, her face was still flushed. Miriam, noticing
her feverish color, said, "Look at your face." She put her
hand to Susanna's cheek. "Burning. Who is it?"

Susanna touched her own cheek and shrugged. "I'm not
sure," she said.

They found a free table by the window and sat down.
The waiter came with menus and sloshed ice water into their

glasses. "You order," Susanna said. She felt she had been talking too much this morning, to herself, and she didn't have the language yet to describe how she felt, even to her closest friend.

"Well, come on," persisted Miriam. "Who is it?"

"Nobody, actually. Maybe I'm coming down with something."

Miriam ordered chicken soup for Susanna, with plenty of chilies; then something soothing made of spinach and cheese. She did most of the talking, telling of her recent exchange trip to Japan to work in a lab outside of Tokyo. Finally both women began to talk of new experiments.

That afternoon in the darkened seminar room, as Susanna showed slides of microscopic insect structures to her colleagues, she kept fingering the neckline of her sweatshirt to make sure the lace straps of her stolen nightgown hadn't migrated. She blushed all through her lecture and was grateful for the darkness.

At night, after putting Robin, her two-and-a-half-year-old daughter, to bed, Susanna peeled off her jeans and shirt, and slept in the rustling dark pink silk.

How does it feel, silk on the skin? It feels like a cat's fur without the fur, or velvet without the nap. It feels like air on a warm night, when you can't tell where you leave off and your surroundings begin.

It has to do with the fineness of the thread. The exact diameter of the silk strands—there are two of them as they come out of the spinneret on the head of the caterpillar—is not important here. We're not used to feeling thicknesses that small, or visualizing thinnesses that great.

Think of it this way: imagine your hand on the mane of a horse. The flanks of a cow. Now caress something finer: a cat, a long-haired one if possible, an angora. As much finer still is the silk thread used in weaving. Touching one such strand gives no pleasure. Just as playing with one cat hair is of no interest. You need the whole pelt.

The reason can be found in your fingertips. Look at them. Look at the thinness of the grooves that make up the finger-print—what if the sensory nerve endings in the fingers are spaced as closely as those grooves? Then anything that thin will be maximally felt. Things much thinner, you won't feel at all. Blow on your fingertips, with your lips pursed as if for whistling. Silk can feel like that.

Susanna's husband Robert had left her in January. Or they had left each other. Separation was their New Year's resolution. He was a painter in acrylics: he still did occasional portraits, but was lately more involved with tall thin canvasses showing edges, borders, doorways. Finally he painted himself out of the picture, leaving Susanna, their baby daughter, Robin, and the girl from Jamaica, Mailys, who was renting a room.

Wait. That was too glib. It wasn't that he painted himself out. Rather, at the same time that his painting was getting better, and going much deeper, Susanna's research with silk-worms was inhabiting her more. They grew to resent each other's differences. She found him too wild and self-indulgent, too aggressively against science. Whenever he found an insect in the house, he would shout that she had brought it from the lab. She was too practical, he said. He felt suffocated by her practical concerns. He accused her of growing a carapace like one of her insects. "You never bother to feel things," he drilled at her, "You're never touched by anything." They didn't see eye to eye; they barely looked at each other. Early September was the last time he had painted Susanna's nude portrait. In the painting she came out looking tall and narrow and rather dark, like his doorways. In fact she was short and broad and had skin like ivory. It was the first time they didn't make love afterward.

Mailys had arrived just after that, to board with them while she finished high school in Boston. Contrary to Susanna's expectations, the girl's astonishing dark beauty had not disrupted family life. If anything, Mailys's calm presence buffered their mutual sharpness, slowed the disintegration of the marriage. Of course, Robert had wanted to paint the young girl's portrait. Mailys decided against sitting for him in the nude, so he sketched her clothed, later painting over the clothes with umber-colored washes. Reversing the classical process of starting with a drawing of the underlying anatomy, he progressively disrobed her on his canvas.

All during that winter of the marriage, Susanna's friend Miriam had been in Japan. Susanna had missed her strong opinions, her bossiness, her willing ear and sharp tongue.

In January Robert had moved out, taking with him his paint messes and his rages. And, yes, his brilliant outbursts and insights. Fleeing Cambridge, he went to visit friends on the west coast. Except for his phone calls, every few days, to talk to Robin, Susanna was left with eddies of quiet. For three months now she'd had order and peace and schedule; she was in the lab by 8:30 each morning. Her research and her child absorbed her energies. Mailys was off visiting colleges.

In the lab Susanna and her colleagues worked with the eggs, caterpillars, pupae and adult moths of Polyphemus, the giant oak silk moth, and of *Bombyx mori*, the mulberry silkworm. They didn't consider silk. They never noticed it. It had nothing to do with their research. The silken cocoon, they slit apart to get at the pupa inside; the pupa, they cut open to get at the eggs; the eggs, they cut up to get at the secrets of development: how do two hundred genes turn on and off and construct the exquisite architecture of this insect eggshell.

For years Susanna had been dissecting moths and then cutting the eggs under a low power microscope with tiny iridectomy scissors meant for eye operations on humans. The pieces she would put into fixative for microscopy, or she would extract them with organic solvents, or tag them with radioactive markers. Each procedure was toxic. Everything smelled bad. If she got too close, the fixatives would kill the cells inside her nose, or the corneal cells covering her eyes. The solvents would act on her brain. She worked with gloved hands inside a fume hood. She had learned not to sniff the ambient air, but to mostly exhale, and never to touch anything with bare skin. Even the black soapstone surface of her lab bench had to be protected with absorbent plastic-backed paper.

Working with Polyphemus, the giant moth with transparent "eye spots" and wavy designs of mauve and tea and sienna on its wings, and black feathery antennae, Susanna felt ugly and ungainly. Although she could dissect with delicate precision, too much of her life right now seemed to be chopping things to bits, this moth of extreme beauty, and its smaller cousin, Bombyx, who could spin unbroken silk fibers a kilometer long.

The idea of silk—as a fabric—was now constantly with her, as though perched on her shoulder like a parrot, nibbling and chattering into her ear whenever she wasn't busy enough.

From the lab tool-drawer, Susanna borrowed a pair of yellow-handled snub-nosed pliers. She started carrying them in her purse when she went shopping, so she could unclip the magnetic anti-thievery tags from the piece she wanted and tack them onto other clothing hanging in the dressing rooms. That way she didn't have to leave the tags lying about.

She began to dress more carefully so as not to call attention to herself in the boutiques. She tucked her clothes in, and brushed her shoulder-length bushy black hair. She powdered her face, though when she thought of the particles of powder resting there, adhering to her skin, her cheeks would twitch. She tried some lipstick her mother had insisted on giving her, but found herself licking it off and wondering whether all red dyes were poisonous. She bought Chanel #19 and dabbed it on pulse points and intimate places.

Any silk would do. She took remnants of almost transparent yellow; lacy peach-colored teddies; slips; nubbly jackets made of the "waste silk" spun from scraps of broken cocoons. She made off with shirts of the silk from the huge Indian Tussah moth, rough-woven in colors of wheatfield and desert.

Susanna perfected a sort of drop-bottomed box, covered in elegant paisley gift wrap, bound with gold ribbons which appeared to tie it shut, but which actually left the underside free to be untucked. On days when she used it, she made sure to leave her purse open-mouthed for the cashier to see into, as though she had nothing to hide. She kept the lab pliers in a green brocade cosmetics pouch, so they wouldn't seem odd. She always purchased something—a scarf or a pair of outrageous socks. Once she even paid for a red silk blouse, but the transaction seemed to rob the blouse of its appeal for her. She gave it to her mother.

Susanna stole slowly and methodically over the course of several weeks. She was charming and cheerful to saleswomen. She was never caught, not even suspected. From time to time she would come to, and question herself sharply. Why, Susanna? Why are you doing this?

In the lab she still wore cotton and denim, covered in a starched white lab coat with the name "Union Linen" in blue cursive script stitched above the breast pocket. Under it all was silk.

One morning Susanna was sitting at her lab desk, surrounded by stacks of photographs and books and lab notebooks with black and white speckled cardboard covers. She had been plotting the day's experiments. Her lair seemed disorderly, but she claimed she knew where everything was. Miriam, whose desk was in the same alcove, was always urging her to try new, more modern, ways to arrange things. Miriam had just given her a set of futuristic file folders in different shades of grey, a present from her recent trip to Japan. Susanna was wondering what to put in them when the lab door slammed.

Takis, a post-doc from Athens, burst in. "Susanna, Miriam—which of you will satisfy my desires today? Who is my destiny?—Or do you say 'whom'?"

"Fuck a rock, Takis," called Miriam.

"You're right, Angel-face, a rock would have more feeling. In that case, do either of you have any sterile saline?"

Susanna gestured to the shelves above her lab bench.

"O-Hai-O, good morning, good morning." Bungo Takaguchi, the post-doc who had come back from Japan with Miriam, came up to their desks and bowed. A small canary-yellow towel hung around his neck. He smelled of soap and toothpaste, faintly geranium-flavored. Although Miriam and Bungo were lovers, he preferred to sleep each night on the couch in the seminar room. First thing in the morning the lab kitchen smelt of soy sauce and sesame oil.

Takis sauntered back again, drumming his knuckles on the top of a rubber icebucket. "Susanna," he called. "Have you given up thinking about your wretched husband? Are you ready for me? I always told you you'd get bored with marital sex."

"The sex was fine," Susanna said. "It was the marriage I couldn't take. What is it with you guys today?"

"It is well known," said Dinakar, a middle-aged professor visiting from Bombay, "that the newly separated or divorced give off pheromones. In any gathering you may watch for it." He got off his high lab stool and walked over to Susanna and

Miriam, waving his pencil like a pointer, eraser end toward the women, saying, "The males will hover around the female—who may not even know she is receptive. I, too, find myself not immune, in this case. However, I am feeling old today." He paused to put his pencil back in his breast pocket, where he patted it to make sure it was secure. "My hormones have drained down to my toes. I think it is due to the hibernation factor. Please wait for me in the springtime. Now, perhaps you should take advantage of one of the others."

Takis set down his icebucket and began to poke holes in the ice chips for his plastic test tubes. "Dinakar's right. Take advantage of me."

"And your wife?"

"My wife just got into the school of veterinary science. She is only interested in small animals. I am yours. Cool me. I itch; I burn."

"Skin disease, Takis," said Miriam. "Have you been swimming where you shouldn't?"

"Metaphor, my dear."

"Takis, none of us would touch you," said Miriam, sadly. "We know all of you too well: to us you're all functional eunuchs."

Brian, a sweet-faced youth from Indiana, strode down the central aisle between the desks and the lab benches. He stopped near Susanna, freeing his blond ponytail from his collar. Since Susanna's separation from Robert, Brian had brought her a loaf of bread each week. Opening his knapsack he took out a dark loaf wrapped in plastic and placed it on top of her lab notebook. He said, "I've just finished all the experiments for my thesis; and all my coursework. I've decided it's time to ask women out.

Would you like to go to the symphony on Friday?"

"Brian, angel, I can't. I'll tell you who to take, though."

"What kind of bread is it?" asked Miriam, sniffing the plastic, as though Susanna's answer should depend on the recipe.

"Buckwheat with raisins."

Susanna knew that the randiness of the lab was simply a function of early morning. Within an hour, their sex and desires, her reluctance to encourage them, would be forgotten or sublimated into pipetting exquisitely small amounts of liquid from one vial to another. The centrifuges would be humming.

The thing about silk next to the skin is this: your body doesn't turn off to it in the same way it does to other materials. Of course your skin can't stay conscious of everything it's wearing, after a while there's a forgetfulness. But with silk the body wakes up each time you shift position, and it says to you, Ah, me, there.

One evening, Miriam brought pizza to Susanna's house. After dinner, they played with Robin and she chased them finally into the room that had been Robert's painting studio. His canvasses and brushes were gone, but heaps of rags remained, as well as paint dribbles on the floor and smudges of charcoal on the walls. An odor of acrylic paint lingered, milky and fermented.

"It's clear what has to happen to this garbage heap," said Miriam.

That weekend, with the help of Miriam and Takis and Brian, Susanna scrubbed Robert's spoor out of the studio. Meanwhile, in the kitchen, Dinakar took over. He made a vat of curried lentils, and cooked carrots with cauliflower, and green things with a peculiar lingering smell.

The next weekend they washed the walls and painted them light yellow to entice the wan spring sun. Susanna began to feel active relief at no longer being married. The pounding needs of Robert's genius, the selfish percussions of his muse—these, in the end, had been more than she could handle. Never marry anyone whose mission is greater than yours is, she thought, or whose muse is more insistent.

Calm breathed into her. Robert had claimed she didn't know how to feel. She took her mug of coffee into the empty room that had been his studio. In the silence of that emptiness, Susanna became aware of noises. In the sun of mid-morning, she could hear the wooden shingles of the house exhale.

Perhaps it had to do with wearing silk.

Your skin has to forget it is wearing clothes, or else too much thought is taken up with the sensations of that vast surface area of your body. If it doesn't forget—you can go crazy: each of your arms feeling its sleeves, the slight tightening at where the button holds the cuff, the extra density down the front of your shirt associated with each button and button hole, the doubling or quadrupling of material around the neck. Your scalp senses how your hair bushes, and where it hits the ears, then prods down to your shoulders. You can evoke it, the consciousness of skin, when you are reminded like this, but you have to keep trying or it lapses.

Susanna, though, didn't have to try; her skin no longer lapsed into forgetfulness. She had grown sensitive to sounds as well as touch. When she went to see friends who studied mating in cicadas, in a lab over in the Zoology Museum building, she would hear not just the cicadas drill, but the slight tweak when they shifted their wings, then the elastic-band flutter and click when they launched into their ornithopter-like flight. On the path leading from the Museum back to her lab, it wasn't the gravel crunching, the slurred, chopping, stone-against-stone sound that she listened to, but the sigh the pebbles gave when they were released from the compression of her foot. She could hear the molecules of stone relax.

There was a man walking ahead of her on the path, a physicist she knew slightly who came to biology seminars. She could see the air around him closing where he had been, and opening up where he was now, the way the space around Robert, who was gone, was now closing in. She had painted Robert out of his studio, and had filled his space in her bed with silk.

"OK, Su. You need a man," said Miriam, who often thought of sex as a universal solution.

Susanna was staring at the page-shaped dark spaces between photographs stacked on the seminar room table. She could hear Bungo's iron teapot cooling and caving in on itself.

"I don't know, I like the quiet."

"It's too quiet. You're listening to things you shouldn't."

Susanna looked up, startled. "What makes you say that?"

"You've got that alert air, when nothing's going on. You're spooky. Besides, you've been out hunting; you've been wearing perfume, clothes."

"I'm not lonely; I don't think. The hunting is something else. Listen. I don't know how to explain this." She told Miriam about the silks. She pulled up the bottom of her sweater to reveal an eggplant-colored teddy.

Miriam whistled like a construction worker, then shook her head, saying, "Even your perversions are old-fashioned."

"How do you mean?"

"Hyphophilia. Fiber lust. A mania of Frenchwomen in the early part of the century. They would steal silk from the Parisian department stores. But then they'd get caught masturbating with it in the elevators."

"Fiber lust. How do you know this?"

"This is the kind of thing I know."

Susanna said finally, "But I don't use it for sex."

"Well, then. For what?" asked Miriam.

Susanna found she could no longer throw out the empty cocoons from the moths she worked on. She had jars full of the sandy brown oak-moth cocoons, and boxes of the smaller finer ones from the commercial moth Bombyx mori—pure white, pale yellow, and bright canary cocoons. Takis came by her lab bench one day and laughed at her, "Thinking of doing some weaving, Susanna?" That was something one didn't do: play with silk.

It wasn't clear what she was ever going to do with them, they couldn't be reeled. The whole point of Bombyx's cocoon is that it's made of a continuous strand of silk, which you unwind after dissolving the glue that holds it in place. But once you've cut through a cocoon, as they had for their experiments on the pupae, the strand is broken up and can no longer be reeled. Still, she kept them.

When Susanna left the lab in the afternoon to pick up Robin, the paths across the campus would holler at her. Her silk underthings rustled and shrieked until she reached the gray house of the day care center and opened the door to the scaled-down world of the toddlers' room. There the red, blue, and yellow of the walls would quiet her own noises. Robin would run to her and jump into her arms, anchoring her solidly.

At home, they would play together on a sheepskin rug she had put in Robert's empty studio. They would chase each other and giggle and pretend to be wild animals until finally the silliness and the laughter had let them unwind from their day's work. Then they would go to the kitchen, where Robin would sit up on the counter while Susanna chatted to her, explaining what she was cooking. After supper and bath and bedtime, and Robin's few lingering calls and questions as she neared sleep, then—the quiet of the house descended.

What were the sounds that Susanna heard once her husband

had left? What is it that we hear when the noisy ones who surround us are hushed? We hear our hearts beating. It's not only our skin that we feel, then, but also our pulse, clocking off the allotted integers. Perhaps the reason that she was hearing these all-too-fine noises was that she didn't want to listen to that clock. She was just thirty. She was listening for the stunning silence, the rapidly filling envelope around a bell when it stops clanging.

Was it only the jibbering noise of mortality? Everyone hears that sooner or later. Susanna may have been trying to hear the noise of the universe. The language in which the world speaks to itself. But like the skin's too-conscious state, these noises are not for mortals, or not for long. Winds that coalesce from nothingness. These are the noises we hear in the desert.

Susanna's bed was full of silks. So were her closets and dresser drawers. Only when she was alone did she allow the silks to show; otherwise she wore them hidden under several layers. She preferred people to see her in sweatsuits. The squareness of her body deserved cotton, she thought.

She brought a man home with her one weekend. Robin had gone to visit Susanna's mother in the neighboring town of Belmont. Jack was a physicist interested in questions of biological form. Sitting beside her in seminar one afternoon, he had seen an errant bit of lace under her t-shirt.

He brought her chocolates in the shape of sea animals: sea horses, fishes and clams. They ate all the sea horses, drank some wine and jumped into bed. As they were scrambling around each other, Susanna's feet touched a pile of silks that she had forgotten to take out of the bed. All through the love-making she was trying surreptitiously to kick these objects into a far corner. When it was over she stretched her feet to feel edges of lace and areas of silken coolness.

On a Saturday in early May, Susanna invited Miriam to cook lunch with her. She had suddenly felt like immersing herself in the smells and textures of the kitchen, and had loaded Robin into the Toyota and driven to Chinatown where they had bought odd-shaped and pungent vegetables.

In the kitchen, Susanna carved a sweet potato into a turtle and gave it to Robin. "Don't eat it; it's not cooked, OK?"

Robin took the potato and walked it across the kitchen floor, making damp oval prints. The women chopped vegetables, ginger, garlic.

"Well," said Miriam. "How's the silk business? Ready for retail?"

"Oh, Lord. I don't know. It's not funny," she said mournfully. "What should I do?"

"What's the latest?"

"It's the one I showed you last week, the yellow slip."

"Then it's slowing down. I wouldn't worry about it; these things often stop on their own."

"What am I going to do with the pieces?"

"Keep them. Use them to lure some more unsuspecting gentlemen."

"I don't want any more gentlemen. Jack is just fine."

"Give some to Mailys, or to your mother. She's your size. Give some to me, I can take them in." Miriam was quite competitive about girth, being small and trim where Susanna was broad.

"Mailys already has lots of silk stuff. I can't give too much to my mother, she'd think it really odd. Besides, it would be making her an accessory after the accessories, a receiver of stolen silks." She giggled and felt immediately weepy.

"Keep slicing," Miriam said. "You can't have too much ginger. We'll think of something. You could..." she paused, and smiled, waving her cleaver in the air. "You could always put it all in shopping bags and take it to the Quaker Meeting House for their clothes lift to Central America. Think of the immense joy of some Salvadoran peasant woman in your purple slip." She rinsed a bunch of scallions and pulled off the wilted leaves. "Of course," she said, looking up for a moment. "You could simply learn to wear them."

In mid-May, Robert called to tell Susanna he was back in town. He wanted to see Robin, he said. He wanted to see Susanna. The moment she heard this she felt sweaty and cold, propitiatory and wanting to be cuttingly rude. She hadn't realized he could still cause such a reaction in her, but she felt as though she was talking to the inquisitor, the inspector general, the heart surgeon. Her ribs caved in; she stuttered. "Why don't you come for dinner," she suddenly heard herself saying. She didn't want to see him, but she wanted to present herself to him.

On a steaming hot Saturday he came and took Robin on

an expedition to his apartment. He would return for dinner.

She spent the day cleaning the house and cooking for him: a curry of lamb with cardamom seeds—a recipe from Dinakar in the lab. She cut orange tulips from her garden and arranged them in a stoneware vase which she placed in the middle of the round oak table. Noticing an old smear of Robin's applesauce on one of the ball-and-claw feet of the table, she took a sponge and a dull knife and sat on the floor to clean it off. Then the other claws looked darker, so she sponged them as well.

In a long slow bubble bath smelling of sandalwood, she rubbed her rough skin with a loofah. She worked on the pads of her fingers, sanding the skin with pumice as she did before an experiment, to make them more sensitive for dissections. When she got out of the tub, her fingertips looked pink and shiny, like Robin's. She ran them over the surface of her towel which now felt thorny and foreign. As she slathered her legs with body lotion, she realized that she was going through a perverse courtship ritual. She needed validation from Robert. She wanted him to state that she was different, now. She wanted him to want her. Then she could refuse him. She would have to—life together had been suffocating for both of them. But at least she would be sure that she was not as numb as he had claimed.

The fragrance of spiced lamb filled the house. She would light candles; she would dress, top to bottom, in silk.

Robert rang the front door bell at exactly seven. Susanna had never known him to be on time before. With Robin in his arms, asleep, he kissed Susanna a bit clumsily and said, "I'll just put her to bed, shall I?"

Susanna waited for him in the kitchen. She lit the candles, shifted the tulips to the side of the table, checked the rice. She hadn't worn outer things of silk before. Too visible. She wished she had started with someone who didn't know her well. She tugged at the waistband of her long skirt, smoothed the sheer yellow blouse she wore on top. As in some shame-filled nightmare, she felt both overdressed and naked.

When Robert came into the kitchen, she couldn't really look at his face. They both started to speak and then backed off.

"I gave her a bath at my place," he said, finally. "With some baking soda. She had prickly heat. First of the season. But what were you about to say?"

Susanna nodded, surprised that he had known what to do, and not wanting to comment on it. "I just wanted to know..." she began awkwardly, then forgot what she had wanted to say. She covered this by asking, "Something to drink?"

All through dinner she felt odd, as though she was moving through familiar landscape, but the native language had been wiped out. They both started to talk at the same time. It was as though each of them could only bear to speak under cover of the other, and it was hard to weave their disjoint utterances into conversation.

She took their empty plates to the sink, feeling her skirt around her calves. She walked to the cupboard to get more candles, still conscious of the sway of the material.

"Come sit here with me," he said.

She sat. He reached over and held her wrist. She was startled by the sweetness of his touch.

"I wonder what it would be like," he said.

"What?" She was stalling, caught off balance by a flaring of desire. She had not expected to want him.

"After four months of not seeing each other," he said.

She hesitated, realizing that she did not want him to know where her clothes had come from. That was too private. She was suddenly afraid he would notice she was in silk. She didn't want him to even mention it. She went completely still inside.

He began stroking her forearm. She put her hand on his, to stop it. "You know," she said. "It really wouldn't be a good idea. It would just cause trouble."

He stiffened and drew back. "Always the cool-headed one. You don't change, Susu, do you?"

His words closed over her and for a moment Susanna felt as though they would drown her in sadness. She and Robert had resumed their very old argument; she knew it would recur whenever they met, now. It would block them from the strangeness of seeing each other clearly, and also protect them from the terror of being seen. It would keep them completely separate.

The beeswax candles flickered in the warm breeze from the window over the sink. The wavering light glinted off the saucepans and cast two shadows, almost overlapping, on the ochre glow of the wall. Susanna adjusted one of the candlesticks and the dark figures danced away from each other. Running her fingertips over the grain of the wooden table she could feel the slight ridges of the continuously alternating seasons.

Borrowed Scenery

AFTER WE HAD DISCUSSED SILKWORMS, AOKI WOULD TELL US about gardens: "In certain Japanese gardens," he would say, "we use the form of a distant tree or mountain as though it stood within the boundary of the garden. We call this process *shakkei*, or 'borrowed scenery.' When the faraway tree behaves as a visual element of the near garden, we say it is 'captured alive.' The design of the garden should allow the tree to continue to live, both within and without."

But perhaps I should begin more at the beginning.

I was in Japan that summer to work on silkworms and to escape marriage, or at least to put it off for a while. I tended to marry too quickly; later would come the slow disentanglement. I was in my late thirties and I'd had a child with each of my three husbands, a girl and two boys. My own mother always preached caution in marital arts, and I was just learning to listen. She and my stepfather took care of my brood while I was away.

Though I rarely get out of my lab in Cambridge, I have

always loved to travel. "I don't want to die before seeing Mongolia and Tierra del Fuego," I told my last husband, Marty. He didn't want me to go anywhere. Though my sample size is small, I think husbands never do. That's another reason I went away that summer: to get wandering out of my system for a while, because Amos had asked me to marry him; he wanted to move in with me and my children, and I wasn't sure what to do. I chose Japan because I also felt the need to be shaken, knocked off balance.

Miriam and I were working for two weeks in Fukuoka on the southern Island of Kyushu. She knows silkworm genetics better than anyone else in the States. I don't know any genetics. I study insect form. I know how silkmoth eggshells are constructed, also their skin, faceted eyes, wings. When, on the green phosphorescent screen of the electron microscope, I uncover the crystalline arrangements inside these structures, it's as though I'm borrowing that order for a while, for myself. Silkmoths, structures—they take me out of myself, out of the chaos.

Married life had never been an ordered arrangement for me. My second husband, Jack, was sweet, and wildly needy, like me. With an ego like a black hole. For a year I told him he was the best theoretical physicist in the world. My saying it seemed to fuel him. When my capacity gave out, when I couldn't utter it any more, he found one of his graduate students who could.

Even Marty, my third one, wanted to be convinced he was best. Carpenter. He was very large. The contrast of his hulking frame and his frail innards still amazes me. When I jumped into marriage with him I took up weight-lifting and eating oatmeal. I didn't get skinny, I'll never be that, but I did get stronger. The marriage got weaker, though, and lasted just long enough for me to conceive his child.

Somehow with each of my husbands, I went terribly wrong, right from the beginning. Blind with love, I forgot the necessary questions. I filled up with reverence. I wasn't even aware that a courtship was going on. I turned sweet, complacent, and dreamy. I sewed curtains for the bedroom. Waking up, I found myself married. Then, a couple of years or months later, a suffocating urgency would engulf me, and I'd have to climb out. It wasn't their fault; how would you like a wife who seemed to prefer silkworms?

When I write up an experiment, it's easy to keep to a single line of thought. With humans, though, and with the self, I have great trouble following any one thread through the disorder. I don't know whether it's more like cat's cradle or like a snarled ball of string. Insects are what I see clearly. Scientific articles are written in third person passive. 'Seventeen female moths were dissected...' That keeps the self and all the people out of it.

But I am trying to tell about Aoki and his silkworms and his gardens.

Kyushu: Miriam and I had a grant to work there, looking for mutations in silkworm eggshells, looking for anything odd. Aoki wanted us to teach his assistant, Jun-Ichi, how to clone silkworm genes. In return, we got to study Aoki's collection of genetically bizarre silkmoths.

From my window in the Foreign Visitors' Quarters of the University I could see a bronze statue of a man above the trees. This was my touchstone in the foreign landscape. Atop a slender pillar a hundred feet high, held in the palm of a mammoth bronze hand, the bronze man balanced on one foot, leaning backwards with his arms stretched wide—for dance or prayer.

Most of the men I knew didn't dance, although Amos claimed he was part dervish. That had still to be tested. Only Robert, my first husband, ever prayed—when he was in the middle of a painting his moods were not under his control. When he wasn't painting, he was impossible. I hardly ever argue with anyone—I usually just slink away and plot hideous revenge—but Robert could provoke me into fights as colorful and monumental as his canvasses.

Still on Eastern Daylight time, I would get up at five A.M. Outside my window, above the green bronze man, stretched layers of cloud just beginning to glow with a warm light. Below breathed the garden of the empty campus: a stream, jagged rocks, a tangle of yellow jasmine.

I made breakfast on the gas ring in my room. I grilled toast directly on the flame, covering the bread with slices of cheese, tilting it to keep the melt from oozing onto the burner. Then I boiled water for instant espresso—Robin had given me a small jar of it as a going-away present, saying, "You never know, Mom." Ten year-old girls can be very wise.

As I sat cross-legged on my bed, smiling at the sharp black taste of coffee, photographs in black and white lay scattered about—all showing the layered crystals that make up insect wings and eyes and eggshells. Except for the one of Amos. Without telling me, he had slipped it in among my micrographs before I left. He's a historian and hates to leave home except for pilgrimages to the great libraries. We had known each other for six months. I had gotten cautious after the painful ending of my marriage to Marty, and I hadn't invited Amos to move in with me, although my children were urging me to ask him.

In my room, I was going to tape Amos's picture to the mirror above my bureau, but I realized I'd see it more often if I shuffled it among the insect pictures. Miriam, who thought I was too unworldly, always complained that I never used mirrors. I could look at moths and crystals, but mirrors were hard to focus on.

"You know, you really ought to take a look occasionally," she prodded. "Your eyebrows, for example."

I thought they were rather original, converging in bushy black cowlicks.

"Well," she said, studying my face. "You could shave them off and start again." Then she would comment on my hair. Women can be quite frank about each other's hair and Miriam didn't hold much back. "You know, nobody wears hair that long and frizzy any more, Susanna. It went out with the Pre-Raphaelites. You'll frighten the Japanese—and the moths." The moths have long feathery antennae of their own.

Miriam was small and sleek. She had just turned thirty and adamantly proclaimed that she would only marry at the last possible moment. "Give me ten more years without clutter," she would say. She always seemed sure of what she wanted.

In my room, checking from time to time on my bronze man, still dancing in front of the blushing clouds, I worked through the dawn silence.

Until the phone rang.

Probably my mother and the kids. At this hour they would just be getting home from school. My mother feared I was never coming home, and hoped to sway me by having them talk to me. This was silly; I'd always been scandalously responsible. I didn't feel my two-week absence was wrong. I missed the children more than I knew how to explain to her. Robin would talk to me of ballet—I was pleased by the ordered movements she was learning; CJ would boast of rockets high over the neighbor's chimney; Charlie, who had learned how to use matches, would have ignited new fires in the garden.

Sometimes Amos would be on the line instead:

"Susanna—my love, my angel, my worm-keeper—how do you grill bluefish? Outside, I mean. Will it stick to the wires? Will it fall apart?"

Late afternoon in Cambridge, he would be standing on his balcony, stretching the phone cord from the living room. I felt it was a good sign, that Amos liked to cook. He was certainly good with the children. Perhaps he could dance after all. I told him how to do the fish and didn't mention where else he could have found the same information. I liked to hear his voice. A brief stab of jealousy, as I wondered who he was cooking for. I wondered if I ought to sabotage the meal and advise him to do it naked on the grill for forty-five minutes.

Miriam would bang on my door, and we'd set out to walk to the lab, dodging bicycle delivery boys and shopkeepers hosing down the sidewalks. Sometimes we dawdled, stopping to take photographs. Once, when we went down a side street the morning quiet was broken by a loud human wailing. A group of mendicant monks were pacing slowly toward us, wearing dark blue jackets over white pantaloons, sandals made of rope, and basket-weave hats down their shoulders. "Woe! Woe!" they seemed to be calling. Housewives darted out to drop coins in their begging bowls.

Miriam wanted to stop and interview the monks, see what their morning "take" had been, and ask them if they had sexual yearnings. I told her they weren't allowed to talk to women, least of all her.

The Sericultural Institute was Aoki's domain. He was tall and thin, with an occasional knowing smile. Unlike most Japanese men, he wore his hair long, almost to his collar. Our first morning there, a Sunday in late May, he bowed us into his empty building, greeting us with almost accentless English. He spoke slowly as if recalling each word from a great depth. Even Miriam was awed; she became proper and polite.

When we had changed from our street shoes into lab slippers, he ushered us in to see his nursery. A humid breeze came through the open windows. The growing-rooms were layered floor-to-ceiling with shelves of flat bamboo baskets.

Silkworms, light and green, glow from within like jade. They eat joyfully—mulberry leaves. Constantly changing, they shed their skins as they grow, finally spinning mile-long silk threads to protect themselves during metamorphosis.

Their life cycle is so orderly that I have always envied them. They change their skin exactly four times before they spin their cocoon. They have to, because their skin is their skeleton, and although it unfolds, it doesn't grow once it is laid down. The worms get swollen and shiny as the old skin is stretched to its fullest, and the new one, highly folded, is made ready underneath. Spinning a bit of gossamer from spinnerets on their heads, they anchor their hind legs to these strands. Then they split the old skin and crawl out. They always know what to do.

Each of Aoki's baskets contained a different strain of the Japanese silkworm *Bombyx mori*. Some of the worms were smooth, some had knobs or hairs. Some were lime-yellow, or had half-moon markings on each segment, or black stripes. Aoki picked up one type of worm and stroked it to show us how it curled into a ball. When you touch the adult females of this strain, he said, they fold their wings and keel over.

The soft yellow light coming in from the mulberry grove outside, the smell of the bamboo baskets and the piles of fresh-cut leaves made an atmosphere of spring forest. When, at one point, we all stopped talking, I could hear the tiny chewing sounds of mandibles on leaves, reminiscent of the singing intake of breath and milk of an infant suckling.

Our work at Aoki's took place in an upstairs room, overlooking the mulberry grove. Mulberry leaves are the only food that the Bombyx silkworm will eat. In Cambridge we didn't grow our own trees, instead, we hunted and gathered. Vacant lots and parking lots often had bird-sown bushes; the magnificent old mulberry at the Botanical Gardens apartments had been killed by Hurricane Gloria, but two large trees still overhung the running path at Fresh Pond. On warm damp evenings I could find new mulberry trees by the smell. Once I had boasted of this to Miriam. She was not impressed. "Chocolate is what humans find by the smell, not leaves," she said. "You're changing into a bug."

We worked well together, Miriam and I. We civilized each other and needed each other around. Unlike me, she was clear-headed and prudent about entanglements, even if her talk was unruly or deficient in self-censorship. Japan seemed to have tamed her though—she hadn't shocked any-one at the formal dinners we had attended.

In Cambridge, at the dean's intimate faculty parties, I'd learned to avoid sitting at Miriam's table. Before departmen-tal meals, especially when officials from government granting agencies were going to be there, I gave her little pep talks, or the reverse. Even so, when I saw some innocent guy across the room turn red, pulling back from the table as he spilled his liquor, I knew she'd been at it.

She started by telling him of the "nuptial flight" of the wild American Oak Silkmoth. How, after emerging from the chrysalis they are stimulated by the perfume of oak scent to "call" over great distances to each other.

"They call each other with pheromones," she said. Then she explained about those hormones that act as perfumed messages. Love notes. They pick up these perfumes with their antennae, great black feathery things, infinitely sensitive. Waving them about in the dark they can sense a single mol-ecule of pheromone. They find each other from miles away. "Ah," she stopped her description here, to have a sip of wine. Then, smiling, she went on: "They screw for three days and three nights, while flying, never stopping to eat or drink. Afterwards they come back to earth, lay their eggs, and die. What about you, are you married?"

If the answer was positive, Miriam would ask her dinner partner about his own "nuptial flight." Then she'd lead him into a discussion of size and shape of genitalia, particularly the human male.

Later, innocent-faced, she would ask me: "Would you rather talk politics? Come on. Everyone's interested in genitals—all through the animal kingdom."

I would lecture her on time and place. But men in business suits triggered something in her. All that dark grey.

In Aoki's lab we were looking at egg sheets: pieces of paper, notebook size, on which fifteen moths had laid circular clutches of eggs, a few hundred in each batch. Each egg was about the size of a poppy seed, so we needed low-power dissecting microscopes to see the details. For ten days we looked at silkworm eggs, between us a total of 1,500,000. Trying to catch anything strange.

From one silkworm strain to another the egg color varied: lemon, olive, apricot, plum. But we weren't looking for color, as that came from the yolk or from the developing embryo, and had nothing to do with the genes which determined the eggshell. Nor were we interested in size or shape, for these, too, were properties of the egg. We were after the subtler qualities of the shell—unusual transparence or opacity, or a surface bloom like that on Concord grapes or plums. Also faint grooves, ripples buckling the smooth roundness of the shell.

We took our breaks standing at the window, gazing greedily at the mulberry orchard, easing our backs by rubbing them with our fists, then pummeling each other. The microscopes, built for Japanese, were too low for us. We were afraid of turning into hunchbacks.

Aoki came to see us every afternoon and shepherded us and Jun-Ichi into his office for green tea. I looked forward to these visits, and saved up questions to present to him, like offerings. I told him of any bizarre eggs I had found, but each time he knew them already and could tell me their batch number and location. I found his knowledge startling and vast. Perhaps that's what first attracted me. I soon grew conscious of which room he was in. If he left the building, the whole place would seem dead to me until I heard his voice again. I found myself studying my Japanese grammar books at night.

Jun-Ichi visited us several times a day, ambling in from the next room, an orange towel hanging out of his back pocket. He worked on the genetics of unusual colors of cocoons: the deep yellows and the rare chartreuse greens. He was always worried about being up-to-date.

"May I practise my English with you?" he asked on our first day. "Are you married?"

"I am not," Miriam said quickly. "But Susanna was, already. Many times." She managed to make it sound as though I was damaged goods.

"And you?" I asked Jun-Ichi, to give him practise.

"Oh, no," he laughed. "Not at all. I am too busy with silkworm. No time to hunt for wife. No time to 'call'."

"Susanna thinks Japanese men are the most beautiful in the world," Miriam said. Jun-Ichi preened, sheepishly.

"Especially old-fashioned Japanese men," I said, setting him straight. "It's Miriam who is very modern."

I was continually surprised that we were allowed to work with those egg stocks. Women. Foreigners. Of course we wouldn't have been allowed anywhere near the strains actually used for commercial silk production—those are classified material. But the eggs in front of us were genetically much more interesting, coming from the strangest worms in Japan. Types isolated and bred by Aoki alone and available nowhere else. If the batches he was currently rearing were to take sick, or if the matings or layings should fail, then the eggs which we were handling, poking, breathing on, would be all that was left of his stocks.

"Susanna, Miriam! Do you know the old-fashioned method for telling sex?" Aoki had come to see us, trailed by Jun-Ichi. We asked Aoki what he meant.

"Sex. Gender of the pupa, while it is still inside the cocoon. Sometimes one wants to use the cocoons of male animals for silk, and let mostly females hatch for breeding purposes. But the problem is to know which cocoons have males, and which have females inside. Without cutting them open." The fineness of silk from *Bombyx mori* is due to the continuous, unbroken filaments. To cut the cocoon makes the silk useless for weaving.

"Susanna, you are the only one of us with a wedding ring. May I use it for a moment? I will give it back to you." Aoki, grinning mischievously, held up a piece of white cotton thread, a meter long. Jun-Ichi had a handful of pale yellow cocoons. As I gave my ring—it had been my grandmother's—to Aoki, he said, "Don't worry. Nothing will be destroyed."

He tied it to the end of the thread and let it spin a moment, unwinding. He was standing near the window and as the ring swung back and forth, hovering in the sunlight, it framed parts of mulberry trees and circles of earth and sky. It seemed alternately golden and solid, then fragile and empty and disembodied.

Aoki took one of Jun-Ichi's cocoons. "The ring should be just a couple of millimeters above the cocoon," he said. "If it swings back and forth in a line, the animal inside is supposed to be male; if it spins in a circle, the animal is female."

"Wait a minute," Miriam said. "Do you really believe in this? Even if there were magnetism of some sort, the setup isn't sensitive enough."

"Besides," I added, "the ring is gold."

"This is very old-fashioned," Aoki replied. "I have just found it in a British work, and I thought you should see these old methods. The author is a Mr. W.J.B. Crotch."

Miriam burst out laughing. I was fearing the worst, but her explanation of the word 'crotch' was completely proper.

"Of both men and women?" Jun-Ichi asked.

"Both," replied Miriam.

Because they were almost a year old, many of the egg batches had colonies of mold. And other life as well. Under the dissecting microscope I focussed on a family of mites, transparent rounded creatures like tiny bubbles with legs, clumsily trekking over the surface of the eggs. They reminded me of Charlie, my youngest, who at three is still very round and lumbering.

Sometimes spikes of grey-green mold burst out of a broken eggshell like micro-fireworks. More rarely there was a stand of white feather mold, bobbing and swaying in the wind of my breath. These white fronds made me think of Robin, wearing a costume she had constructed of bedsheets and drinking straws, dancing for me and Amos one night in the kitchen.

We took samples of the unusual eggs to work on back in the States, where we would hatch them, grow the worms, let them spin, emerge as adults, mate, and lay their eggs. I would look for architectural strangeness in the ordered structure of the eggshell, while Miriam hunted for differences in the DNA, chopping it to pieces and searching for indications of how genes are switched on. In the end, these problems all reduce to questions of genes and the proteins which influence them by bonding to them and letting go, questions of attraction.

When I'm in a certain mood, pushing explanations to ever tinier levels of organization can bother me. It reminds me of when I was five years old and would sit on the kitchen linoleum, cutting paper. My mission was to cut a piece of my school workbook paper into nothing-at-all. To thwart my natural sloppiness, I lined up the halves, quarters, eighths, cutting each one in turn. Then, when all the snippets crumpled between the blades, I ransacked my mother's room for sharper, smaller tools. Finally, surrounded by a snow-field of tiny flecks of paper, I saw that my task had become infinite.

At tea on our tenth day in the lab, Aoki unfolded a stack of oversize papers, his intricate breeding plans of genetic crosses for the current season. These diagrams of how individuals should be coupled fascinated me. The white paper was mapped out with red and blue arrows and dotted lines, names of strains and families. He explained to us what he was going to do, moving his fingers slowly from one Japanese name to another. I found myself looking at his long, thin hands, realizing I'd never noticed them before. Watching his tapered fingertips, I forgot all about the genetics. When he noticed that

I wasn't listening, he spoke to me.

"Eh, Susanna-*san*, time to wake up. Look, I'm putting your mutant in here." He smiled as he penned in a bizarre strain of eggs I had found. They were dappled with areas of clear transparence and bloom. A mutation he had not known. I was pleased that something of mine was now inscribed in his plans. How sure he was of his matings and breedings.

As he folded his papers, I wondered if I should ask him what to do about Amos. But Miriam had commented on the view from his window, and he was talking about gardens again:

"The thing to remember," he was saying, "Is that we don't choose just anything to capture alive for our borrowed scenery. Only the most venerable trees, only the most worthy mountains."

Miriam said, "You know, speaking of trees and mountains, we really haven't been able to see much of either. I've still got time, but Susanna has to return to the States in less than a week. Now that she's finished her work in the lab, she needs to go off somewhere to write her paper—don't you think she ought to see the countryside? Don't you know some wonderful spot?"

I was embarrassed by her shameless urging, but pleased when Aoki offered to make arrangements for me to go to an inn owned by a friend of his, deep in the mountains of Kyushu. He said he might pass by for a visit. Miriam was to stay on in Fukuoka to begin some breeding experiments. She was also starting something else, with Jun-Ichi.

It was hard to say good-bye to Aoki. If I'd been sharper-eyed, I would have noticed how weak-kneed and worshipful I had become. As if to rouse me, Jun-Ichi rushed over to shake my hand. He kept on pumping it. The Japanese I met that summer rarely shook hands with me, but when they did, the tempo was highly individual. Often I had time to feel their hands in a way I wasn't used to. It became an embrace. When Aoki did not offer to shake hands, I realized I'd been looking forward to that small contact. Instead, he bowed. I returned his bow, not knowing whether it stood for more or less than a handshake.

I packed my bags that night, as my train was to leave very early. Going to bed I could see the darkening campus and the bronze man, flood-lit and awestruck. He seemed to stagger backwards, as though in flight.

Later, the telephone shrilled me out of sleep. It was 2 A.M.

"Moshi-moshi," I answered, heart pounding. The phone cord was all tangled. Who would call at this hour? Amos didn't like to wake me up, but my mother never hesitated, especially if one of the children had a story to tell.

It was a girl, I thought, on the other end. Japanese. Not anyone I knew. I was relieved. Except that she was in a bad state. Weeping or whimpering. Speaking my primitive Japanese, I haltingly told her the unnecessary facts that I was a foreigner and didn't speak much Japanese. I mean, I could say 'up' and 'down' and 'As for the poisonous puffer fish, please don't give me any.' But if it was to be anything interesting, I couldn't say it. She said some things I didn't understand. I turned on my light to look up the phone number of the superintendent.

"Listen," I said, slowly. "Perhaps you would like to speak to a Japanese person; here is the number of a Japanese person."

But she didn't want that Japanese person, she just wanted to go on talking to me. The cold shock of the deep night call alarmed my heart.

As the conversation continued, I understood even less. Her voice, already quite breathy, grew weaker. I pictured her on a window ledge, on the edge of an abyss, *in extremis*. I had to say something to bring her back. She didn't seem to understand any English at all. I tried to dredge up enough Japanese to calm her. There was no one in that night but us two; even my green man, my friendly statue, was no longer visible. Why such misery? And how had she stumbled on me?

Thinking that perhaps she had known someone who lived in my room, I told her that I was a biologist, that I worked on *o-keiko-san*, the honorable silkworm, and that I had been in Kyushu for ten days. I felt powerless and shaken, realizing that if something happened, if she killed herself, I wouldn't hear about it. Even if I could get my Japanese friends to scour the newspapers, I didn't know who she was, or where she was calling from.

Once more I tried to get her to tell me.

She whimpered and gave a deep sigh. Then silence. My heart thumped as though it wanted out. Her voice shifted much lower and she finally said:

"*Terewhon sekisu, wakarimasu-ka* ?" Telephone sex, do you understand?

I did. It wasn't a 'she' at all. And the *extremis*—well, in my midnight telephone panic, I had mistaken one heightened emotion for another.

"No. Excuse me. I don't understand," I lied, trying to save face. And trying to keep from giggling or bursting into tears. I talked on a little more, and then hung up.

As I double-bolted my door, my hands were shaking. I called Amos—he could always calm night-fears—but it was still lunchtime in Cambridge, and he didn't answer. He would be at a café, French, Italian, or Algerian, drinking espresso with his friends, gesturing and talking.

I slid open the window and stepped out on the balcony. No one was lurking down below. The night was warm and full of mist, the air so thick it felt nourishing. I thought how little I understood the world out there, or even the closer, more hidden world of my own attractions and repulsions, the short-lived bonds I made with my husbands.

At the inn, windows on two sides of my room let in the soft rainlight. A sliding screen opened onto a wild garden of climbing vines and purple thistles. Beyond lay a green rice paddy. The garden on the other side had a tall clump of tasselled grass, a spider web, beaded with the mist. The room smelled of fresh rain and the straw of the tatami mats.

I worked on the data I was analyzing for my paper every morning. Afternoons I would hike in the countryside, photographing temples, shrines, insects. Sometimes I talked with the other guests, but conversation was limited; I was the only foreigner. I couldn't remember ever having been alone before.

Fumiko, the chambermaid, would announce herself and my dinner as she slid open the outer of two sets of doors to my room. In old-style Japanese inns, the maid, in full kimono, serves dinner in your room. At first, I had jumped up to help her each time she came in. She had put me in my place, though, showing me how to kneel, feet neatly under butt. Whenever she left, I would unfold myself, all pins and needles.

I had been there for three days when she told me that Aoki had just arrived. She knew him from his many visits. Very great scientist, she said. He was eating with his friend, the owner of the inn, and had asked Fumiko to find out if I would have a drink with him afterwards. The indirectness of the invitation amused me; I told her I would.

The meal that night centered around obscure plant life, coiled shapes I'd never eaten. Fumiko went over their names, testing me until I got them right: *Zenmai, Warabi, Fuki* and *Seri*. As soon as she left, I took out my *Guide to Eating in Japan*. Those rare seasonal vegetables were Flowering Fern, Bracken, Bog Rhubarb, and Dropwort. They tasted bitter-sweet and fibrous.

In the end of the rain, the breeze whispered through the tangled vines of my garden. Spring peepers joined their high pitched cackles to the throaty drumming of the bullfrogs. Above the tiled roofs, the sky had turned slate blue. Night was coming. Outside, in the forests and paddies, they croaked and chirped and purred.

The outer door slid open and Fumiko said, "It's only me, may I come in?"

I shifted into kneeling position, my back straight. She asked if she should help me get dressed. This flustered me. I wasn't used to the custom of the maids in old-fashioned inns helping guests dress.

"How do you mean?" I asked.

"Well, I thought you might want to wear something differ-ent. You see, often Professor Aoki likes to walk at night. Usually with the innkeeper, but tonight he is busy. Possibly it's the right time for *hotaru*, and Aoki-*sensei* especially likes to walk then."

I understood everything except *hotaru*. It was a familiar word and I ought to have remembered what it meant, but I was embarrassed to ask her to explain.

"As for jeans," I asked. "Would they be OK?"

She helped me dress, then stood back, shook her head and handed me a black silk shirt. I reached for my white jacket but she said, "No, better not. On account of *hotaru*— better something dark." She pulled out a navy sweatshirt. We disagreed about footwear: she was not fond of running shoes. This time I won. My feet felt like they would probably atrophy anyway, from kneeling.

"Are you frightened?" she asked.

"Frightened? Of what?"

"Aoki-*sensei*. He is very wise."

"No. Not at all. I have worked with him."

"Oh, I see." She cocked her head to look at me. But she had knocked me out of my sureness.

"Do something, please, with your face and hair," she told me.

Her own hair was smoothed into a complex, perfect, unfathomable knot. I felt jealous of her knowing how to sit, probably how to live. What if I had the words in Japanese to talk about my three failed marriages, and about my children? What if I were to tell her I was thinking of marrying Amos, and that I was lusting after Aoki?

I didn't say anything. I washed my face and sat quietly as she tied my own hair into a twist, then wrapped it with long red sash.

∞

An hour later the outer door to my room opened, and there was a soft tapping at the inner one.

Finally I got to shake hands with Aoki. I had to put both my hands around his, to make sure he was there. Like a wild moth you want to capture: you want to hold it without harming its wings so all you can do is enclose it, encircle it, and only the slight fluttering, brushing against your palms, allows you to feel you've got it.

"It is good to see you again, Susanna-*san*." He stood in the doorway, silent for a moment, then said, "Ah. Look, would you mind if we take a walk. The rain has stopped and there is something I want to show you." He was wearing a dark kimono with a blue over-jacket, and *geta*, wooden sandals. It was the first time I had seen him in Japanese clothes. He was even taller than I remembered, wraith-like.

We went up a twisting road leading into the foothills of Mt. Aso. Within minutes we had left the last houses of the village behind, the *tok-tok* of Aoki's wooden sandals setting our pace. I had not taken this path in my walks. The frog noises faded; crickets took over.

I followed him up some steps by the side of the road. A small shrine with a flowering azalea nudging a statue in the moonlight—a Buddha dappled with lichens. A large bronze bell loomed under a thatched roof.

"No one lives here any more," Aoki said. "Listen."

He pulled back the horizontal log suspended on ropes beside the bell and then let go. The *bong* when it came was soft and deep-voiced. He swung the log even further and let it fly again; a round booming tumbled down the hillside, generating eddies of sound in the pockets of shadow.

Aoki dropped a few coins in a box beneath the bell and lit incense and candles. As he bowed with joined hands, I wondered what form his prayer took, whether he prayed for someone or to someone. I didn't dare ask. Then he turned to sound the bell once more, softly this time, and we went down the steps back to the road.

We didn't talk very much. Partly, I guess, because the night was still so full of its own noises. His hand alighted on my elbow to steer me off the road and onto a dirt path. The ground was springy underfoot and smelled of earthmold. As we walked into a bamboo grove the moonlight was sieved into prisms, lozenges on the forest floor. Overhead, the leaves rustled, a passing breeze shaking down occasional drops of rain.

"Here," he said. "Touch." Taking my hand, he put it on one of the tree trunks. The bamboo was covered with velvet, like deer antlers. Not all the trees were that way, just some. I forgot to ask him why, whether it had to do with species, or with sex.

The lake surprised me. I hadn't seen it on my map of the region. It wasn't very large, but mist obscured its far shore. Aoki untied a bundle he'd been carrying and spread a dark cloth on a rock at the water's edge. He motioned me onto it and sat down beside me, placing a thermos and two small ceramic cups in front of us. He opened the lid of a wooden bowl of crackers, then poured us each some cold *sake*. We sat there, drinking.

Wild iris in the water by our rock were in bloom but I couldn't tell what color they were: possibly yellow, possibly white. Aoki shifted a bit, and again his dragon-fly hand rested on my arm.

"Look," he pointed. "*Hotaru!*" Into the mist behind the stand of iris darted spots of light, glowing softly, zig-zag, on-off.

"Ah, *hotaru*," I repeated. Fireflies.

I had spent my life studying insects of one kind or another, but had never seen them like that—magnified by the mist, each one surrounded by a halo of diffused light, as large as my hand.

As we sat watching the play of fireflies over the water, Aoki started to sing. At first the noise startled me. It began with a deep-throated growl, a bit more extended than if he were clearing his throat. Gradually it became more melodic as his voice moved into higher registers. But both melody and tempo were Japanese and several times I mistook a pause for the end. Not that I wanted it to be over, it's just that I didn't know where I was in the song. A mosquito took its time biting the back of my neck. I didn't move.

I didn't catch much of the song's meaning, except for some names of insects: *Suzumushi*, the bell insect which has a chiming call; *Matsumushi*, the pine tree insect, and something which sounded like *Tsuku Tsuku Boshi*, which may be a bright green cicada. There was also a sprinkling of women's names. But whether it was one song or many, and whether they were love songs or insect songs, I couldn't say.

He rocked back and forth as he sang, keeping his hand on my arm, and when at last he finished, it was in the same low purring growl with which he'd started.

In the last shudder of the night, just before the first hope of morning, the fireflies disappeared: fewer, only three, then none. No. Now, none. Aoki poured the final drops of *sake* into our cups, offered a silent toast first in the direction of the fireflies, then to me, and smiled.

The next day I set out in early morning for a walk into the hills. The countryside was transformed into full summer. I photographed a bamboo grove, volcanic rocks, a blue and copper striped lizard.

When I got back, Aoki was sitting in my garden, smoking a cigarette. This was odd; I'd never seen him smoke before. You can't when you work with the worms, they won't thrive. He beckoned to me. I sat with him.

"Ah, I could stay here forever," I said, without thinking.

He puffed at his cigarette and didn't reply. Finally he said, "Here in the mountains? Or here in Japan?"

"Both. I guess I mean in Fukuoka... at the Institute."

"No," he replied, suddenly grave. "You must not marry in Japan."

He thought I was proposing to him. I was.

This was how it happens.

Blood rushed to my face, pounded in my ears. I felt sick. How close I'd come again, without thinking. But because he had stopped me at the edge, suddenly I could focus on the past weeks. They were laid out in front of me as though in the field of my microscope, and I could see how I had let myself become over-reverent and under-critical. I had lost my sense of humor and forgotten to question. I hadn't even been able to bat the mosquitoes at the lake. I was still not sure what to do about Amos, but I welcomed that unsureness. It wasn't good for me to lose my head.

Then the pain hit me, of being so bluntly refused by Aoki. Of course he was correct, but reason doesn't stop wanting. Nor did the fact that I would probably marry Amos. Sometimes we are greedy for love. My cheeks were burning and for a while I couldn't talk.

"Tell me what you mean," I said, when I finally got my voice back. Even though he had tried to save me from the embarrassment of a direct refusal, by saying I should not marry *in Japan*, I didn't want to let myself off so easily. If he had a clear view of these things, I wanted to see it.

"In a minute," he replied. Perhaps he needed time as well. "First we shall do something. You go there." He pointed to the tall stand of ornamental grass. There he photographed me, using his camera, and then mine.

"Open your eyes," he said sharply. I had been squinting into the yellow morning sun.

Then we changed places. I took a long time positioning him in my view finder until the ground was level and the golden stalks radiated on all sides, framing him, almost perfectly. I motioned him a little more toward the center.

"Yes... please stay there," I said, exchanging my camera for his.

About the Author

GRACE DANE MAZUR teaches creative writing at Harvard University and Emerson College. Her stories have appeared in the *Southern Review*, the *New England Review*, and *Breadloaf Quarterly*, the *Harvard Review*, and STORY. *Silk* is her first collection of stories. Her obsessions with light and sharpness of focus come from the seventeen years she worked with light and electron microscopes, examining insect structures.